Pe

The Femails

Margaret Clark is the author of more than a hundred books of fiction for children and young adults. She has won numerous local and international awards. She has worked as a school-teacher, a lecturer and a counsellor, and has recently completed a doctorate in education at Deakin University. She lives in Geelong, near Melbourne. *The Femails* is her first novel for adults.

The Femails

MARGARET CLARK

Penguin Books

PENGUIN BOOKS

Published by the Penguin Group
Penguin Group (Australia)
250 Camberwell Road, Camberwell, Victoria 3124, Australia
(a division of Pearson Australia Group Pty Ltd)
Penguin Group (USA) Inc.
375 Hudson Street, New York, New York 10014, USA
Penguin Group (Canada)
10 Alcorn Avenue, Toronto, Ontario, Canada M4V 3B2
(a division of Pearson Penguin Canada Inc.)
Penguin Books Ltd
80 Strand, London WC2R 0RL, England
Penguin Ireland
25 St Stephen's Green, Dublin 2, Ireland
(a division of Penguin Books Ltd)
Penguin Books India Pvt Ltd
11 Community Centre, Panchsheel Park, New Delhi – 110 017, India
Penguin Group (NZ)
Cnr Airborne and Rosedale Roads, Albany, Auckland, New Zealand
(a division of Pearson New Zealand Ltd)
Penguin Books (South Africa) (Pty) Ltd
24 Sturdee Avenue, Rosebank, Johannesburg 2196, South Africa

Penguin Books Ltd, Registered Offices: 80 Strand, London, WC2R 0RL, England

First published by Penguin Group (Australia),
a division of Pearson Australia Group Pty Ltd, 2005

1 3 5 7 9 10 8 6 4 2

Cover and text design by Miriam Rosenbloom © Penguin Design Studio
Cover photograph by Ryan McVay/Getty Images
Cover background Indian textile print from the Pepin Press, www.pepinpress.com
Typeset in 12/18 Joanna by Post Pre-press Group, Brisbane, Queensland
Printed and bound in Australia by McPherson's Printing Group, Maryborough, Victoria

National Library of Australia
Cataloguing-in-Publication data:

Clark, M. D. (Margaret Dianne), 1943– .
The femails.

ISBN 0 14 300189 2.

1. Widows – Fiction. 2. Electronic mail messages – Fiction. I. Title.

A823.3

www.penguin.com.au

To Fe, my daughter,
with lots of love from Mum
(and to David and Curly Lee)

February 7

ATTENTION: LUCY FINDLAY (PRIVATE AND CONFIDENTIAL)

Surprise! It's me – Cath. This is my first ever email to anyone and it's to you, my dearest fiend.

I'm at SPUDS. As you well know, it stands for 'Skills and Processes for Understanding Daily Situations' – not, as you keep telling all our friends, 'Sex and Porno for Universally Deprived Singles'. So please stop it!

Anyway, I feel I've turned the page and I'm glad I enrolled in this course.

Do you mind being emailed at work? The computer tutor told me to put the bit about private and confidential at the top, so no one else reads it.

What was I saying? Oh yes, my memory. I was talking to Pam about forgetting things and she said, 'I know, I always have trouble with the hereafter.' I asked her what she meant by the hereafter and she said, 'I walk into a room and think, What the hell am I here after?'

Fe is somewhere in Turkey and travelling on her own, after her friend Michelle decided to stay in Japan. I'm worried about her. There was a riot in Turkey on the news last night and I could swear I saw Fe standing near a tree. It would be just like her to watch the action instead of ducking for cover. I can hear you snorting, 'She's nearly twenty-three, Cath. She can stand next to a tree and watch a riot if she wants to.'

I hope this trip helps her 'find herself', as you would say, and come to terms with losing her father. I just wish she wasn't travelling on her own – a lot of backpackers seem to get murdered. Of course, I can't be too fearful about all this when I write to her. I have to try to be motherly and calm. But I do wish I could have talked to her more about James's death. I should have been a better mother. If something happens to her, it'll be my fault.

Hope this email comes through okay.

Love as always, Cath

February 7

ATTENTION: LUCY FINDLAY (PRIVATE AND CONFIDENTIAL)

I am so excited. A return email straight into my SPUDS classroom! I didn't realise it would be so fast. Thanks for the tip about using the spell-checker. And thanks for offering to get me the Eternal Life Anxiety Relief pills, though I hope they won't react with all the other naturopathic stuff I'm taking, which still doesn't seem to be working. But I've made an appointment with the hormone specialist you recommended.

Who's Pam? She's in my SPUDS class. Her husband died years ago, and for the last three she's had what she calls 'a gentleman caller' who visits once a week. She refers to him as Mow (Mr Once Weekly). To have that sort of relationship, she says, you have to think like a man and compartmentalise. I can't imagine doing that. Anyway, maybe you and I can have coffee with Pam one day. I'm sure you'll like her. She's practical and sensible, but also fun.

So you think it's all right to tell Fe I'm worried about her, but I shouldn't do it in a carping way? Okay, I'll send her a caring, non-carping email. But I still think I'll ask her about the riot.

Love as always, Cath

February 7

Dear Fe

It's me – Mum. I'm doing this email in my computer class. Have you been watching a riot over there? Someone very like you was on the news last night. If it was you, that was a dangerous and foolish thing to do. You could have been shot. Maybe you're lying injured in some Turkish hospital. This is all extremely worrying, as I have no idea where you are or what you're doing.

I've been thinking. Would you like me to fly over and keep you company? Mind you, it would be a bit nerve-racking, as I've only ever been to New Zealand and that was with your father. But Lucy's getting me some herbal anti-anxiety pills, so I'd be able to cope. If you want me to come, I can drop everything. I'd have to make arrangements for someone to mind Grandma and Grandpa and the garden and the dog and cat, and collect the mail and suchlike. But that's okay, I'll work it out.

Lucy says I shouldn't worry so much about you, but I can't help it. You could be lying under a bridge with your throat cut for all I know. What with grieving for your father and worrying about you, and menopause, I'm a bit weepy and weary. Not that this is meant to make you feel guilty, I want you to enjoy your holiday. But can you try and stay healthy and not go into war zones? Your Great-Granny Potts always said, 'When in doubt, don't.'

If you can't email, then phone. Reverse the changes if you haven't any cash.

Love from Mum xx

February 9

DEAR FE

I hope you don't mind me using your computer. Now I can email from home whenever I like. I was delighted to get your email, though it was rather brief. Relax, I won't fly over to Turkey, but can you please give me the phone number of the hostel where you'll be staying next? I know you dropped your mobile phone in the river, but there must be public phone boxes in Turkey.

Now that I know you're alive and well, I'll tell you the latest news. Tomorrow I have to go to a doctor in Melbourne who deals in natural hormones. Lucy thinks I'm very run-down and over-stressed due to your father's death and getting used to living alone, and coping with Grandma and Grandpa and your being away.

I'm thinking of taking the train, as it's less stressful and only takes an hour. I *could* drive up the highway and get onto CityLink, but I'm a bit worried about the tunnel. I know it comes out somewhere, but where?

And everyone drives too fast, and they keep changing the roads and putting up detour signs. Hardly any of my friends will drive to Melbourne now, they'd rather take the train. Maybe that's what the government wants: if they make the roads horrendous enough, everyone will use public transport.

Must go.

Love from Mum xx

February 11

Dear Fe

I'll try a longer email and make it like a newsy letter. Next week I'm having my umbilical hernia removed. You know how my navel sticks out? Maybe you didn't. Anyway, it's an easy operation and I'll be home in two days. They'll just cut out the hernia and then stitch my navel back together. Please don't worry about me, I'll be fine.

Speaking of stitching, Amy phoned from Sydney and said Dwayne has stitched up another deal. They're doing so well. Of course, being American he has lots of connections. Amy offered to come and look after me when I have the operation, but I told her Lucy had already offered.

Your nieces and nephews are all well. Dakota and Sydney are in the Seascape Day Care Centre now, as Amy felt the other place wasn't educational enough. Dakota's already been moved from Dolphins group to Penguins, and he's not three yet. He's very advanced in everything except toilet training, but I don't suppose you need that to be a doctor or architect or prime minister. He's very good at maths. He knows all his numbers to ten.

Sydney's in Limpets, but he'll move to Turtles when he starts to crawl. He can scoot around on his bottom a bit, but that doesn't count for promotion to Turtles. He turned nine months old on Wednesday, so he should be crawling soon.

Virginia and Georgia are very organised for the first term. They're doing ballet on Mondays, callisthenics on Tuesdays, violin on Wednesdays, netball and tap on Thursdays, swimming on Fridays, and tai chi on Saturdays. Dwayne believes children should be scheduled, but I think it's more of an American thing. He's scheduled himself to go to a conference in Los Angeles in April, and he's taking Amy and the children too.

Virginia and Georgia's mother (you know, Marla) wants them to stay with her for a week. She's between acting jobs right now and she says she'll take them to Disneyland. Dwayne, Amy, Dakota and Sydney will drive down to Orange County and stay with Dwayne's mother and father. I think they're going to Disneyland too. Blended families do get a bit messy, but at least Amy has a reasonably cordial relationship with Marla and her new husband.

It would be nice to drop your sister a line and ask how your nieces and nephews are. When you do, please don't call them those nicknames. You know how it annoys Amy.

Grandpa and Grandma are fine too, although Grandpa keeps trying to phone Parliament House to argue with the prime minister about all things political. Whenever I go to visit, he wants me to drive him down to the Centrelink office so he can argue with them about not standing up for the rights of pensioners. Your poor grandma is forever writing letters that he dictates, about how the country is going to the dogs and how it should be run, but they never get sent because he never finishes them. Grandma reckons he forgets where he's up to and wanders off. Still, it gets things out of his system, I suppose.

Speaking of the prime minister, someone called talk-back radio the other night and said they wanted to hang him by his testicles but they couldn't because he hasn't got any.

Now, don't worry about me, especially my operation. I'll be fine. I'm used to having to manage by myself now. Email me when you can, although I realise this can be difficult if you're not near a computer that's connected to the Internet.

Love from Mum xx

February 13

Dear Amy

Yes, it's your mother writing you an email instead of phoning. I'll keep it short, since it's probably not a good ideal to email you at work. I'm glad Fe emailed you. Yes, she does seem to be having a lot of adventures. Not that I know much about the latest ones, because she hasn't phoned for a while and has only sent the briefest email to say she's alive and well.

I was surprised you said she was worried about my operation, because as I told you, it's nothing dramatic. And there's certainly no need for you to fly down from Sydney, though I do appreciate your offer. You'd have to take time off work and drag Virginia and Georgia out of school and Dakota and Sydney out of day care, and they'd be bored here without their friends and their schedules. Plus they'll be missing school when they go to Los Angeles, won't they? I'll be fine, and with Lucy's nursing background she'll do a good job of looking after me, so don't worry.

Love from your mother x

February 14

DEAR FE

Your general email to everyone just arrived. Who on earth are hotbod, hellz_anjel, sixty_niner and fishguts?

I'm really glad you've made so many new friends travelling, but do be careful. They could be criminals in disguise.

Thanks for the tip about clicking Reply and then Send. I think I hit Reply All by mistake. Never mind, I'm becoming quite computer lateral. And isn't spell chick a help?

Sorry to rush. Have to go.

Love from Mum xx

February 14

ATTENTION: LUCY FINDLAY (PRIVATE AND CONFIDENTIAL)

I've heard from Fe and she wasn't anywhere near that riot, thank goodness. She's travelling through Turkey with some new friends she's made, so I'm happier now I know she's not on her own. But I'm still worried, because she says she's going to out-of-the-way places and not the regular tourist spots. I hope she's had the right injections.

I think you said you're in Brisbane this week, but I suppose you'll get this on your laptop. Email is almost more fun than phoning. I like the fact that you have time to think about what you want to say. I haven't quite figured out a few things on Fe's computer yet, which is different from the one at SPUDS.

According to your Dr Valushi, I'm one of those women with totally depleted hormones. She gave me a script for some new plant hormones. I got it filled and now take Trieste 8 (I think that's oestrogen), progesterone 100, testosterone 5.5, DHEA 3 and another one for my memory, but I can't remember its name right now.

I heard a discussion about natural hormones on talkback and I'm feeling confident they'll work. Apparently they can fix everything: muddle-headedness, aches and pains, insomnia, night sweats, and panic attacks. I hope so. Of course they'll take a while to kick in, and Dr Valushi said she always starts with lower doses to see how people react. I have to have a bone-density scan, too, and maybe get the hormones adjusted after the next blood test. You're so lucky you just cruised through menopause. For me it's a nightmare.

Did I tell you Amy offered to come down with the kids after my hernia operation, to look after me? I couldn't think of anything worse! I know she's my daughter and I should be grateful for her offer, but she'd just waft around criticising everything, and the children would demolish the place. Sydney eats everything in sight, even though he's only got two teeth. Dakota throws things everywhere and fights with the animals, and the girls whine because I haven't got a DVD and computer games.

And you know what Amy's like. 'Mother, you look like a derelict in those tracksuit pants.' 'Mother, there's dust on the ironing board.' 'Mother, nearly all the food in this fridge is past the use-by date.' Everything has to be just perfect. She's always on about wearing the right clothes and having the right friends and not letting one's standards slide.

How I could have two daughters so different, I don't know. They're like chalk and cheese. Fe couldn't care less about impressing people and her room was always a pigsty. Maybe Amy has the right attitude and the right values to get on in today's world, but she intimidates me. Somehow I always feel that I don't quite measure up to her ideal of motherhood.

Helene offered to have me to stay, too. I nearly fell over with shock. She phoned all sugary-sweet and said they'd 'absolutely love' to have me. Translate that as, 'I'm doing my duty and asking you, but heaven forbid you should take up the offer.' She must have been so relieved when I told her I'd made other arrangements. As you know, I never see Helene and Robert from one end of the year to the next. Mum told Robert I was having the operation, so I suppose he thought it was the brotherly thing to do. Can you imagine me clambering up and down all those stairs in their apartment straight after a hernia op?

And Robert would probably present me with a bill for expenses at the end of the stay. He's always been tight with his money, and Helene is a bad influence. She's a two-bob snob, as my dad would say. On the rare occasions they visit Mum and Dad they never bring a thing, not even a bunch of flowers. You'd think they could buy a cake or a cooked chicken or something. I don't know whether it's because they're mean or they just don't think about things like that. Maybe Robert's doing a payback because Mum and Dad didn't send him to a posh private school – you know how he's always had a chip on his shoulder.

Jane and I had a quick lunch at Antipasto's before she leaves for the UK. You're not going to believe this, but she's dyed her hair bright red. It's so over-the-top and not like her at all, which makes me think maybe you're right and she and Derek have marriage problems. You know, doing a make-over on herself to revive the relationship. Perhaps that's why she's going with him this time? Derek usually does those business trips on his own. And they're taking a holiday as well. A second honeymoon? She said she'll send me an address when they get there, as she's not sure whether they'll be based somewhere or be travelling.

Of course I had to say something about her hair, so I said, 'New hair, new you?' And she said, 'So what do you think?' I said, 'Well, it's certainly different,' which was true. But it actually looked ghastly. She was wearing her green suit with an orange scarf and she looked like a set of traffic lights.

Anyway, I'm eternally grateful that you're having me to stay after the op. I've got my own address now – it's cathmo55@hotmail.com. That will get me at home and not at the computer class.

Love as always, Cath

February 16

Dear Fe

What an amazing experience Gallipoli must have been. I didn't realise the coast there is 35 kilometres long, I imagined it as just a small beach. I couldn't find Gelibolu in the atlas, but I did find Canakkale. Your Great-Grandpa Potts was in the First World War, so he was probably at Canakkale. I think your father's side of the family had someone at Gallipoli too. They're all gone now, of course.

I guess we're lucky to still have Grandma and Grandpa Miller alive and well, although Grandpa is losing his sight more and more. Last week he fried some fish in Golden Lights detergent and Grandma thought he was having a seizure because bubbles came out of his mouth.

I'm looking forward to seeing the photos of you beside the big wooden horse of Troy. It's hard to believe that Troy really is a place and not just a legend. Yes, do buy a digital camera if it means you can send photos by email. But this time please don't give it to some stranger to take your photo so he can run off with it, like you did at Gallipoli with your good Konika. Only let them use the throw-away one.

I'll put some extra money in your bank account, but please be careful with your spending, Fe. The probate on your father's will finally came through – it was complicated by trusts and off-shore accounts that I didn't know anything about. I guess your father had his reasons. Anyway, there seems to be a lot of money unaccounted for and this has to be sorted out.

Don't worry about my operation. As I told you, it's simple. It will be just a small cut and then they stitch the skin back together.

Love from Mum xx

February 17

ATTENTION: LUCY FINDLAY (PRIVATE AND CONFIDENTIAL)

Okay, maybe I was a bit cruel about Jane, but if you'd seen her hair I'm sure you'd agree. I couldn't bring myself to tell her to her face, though. You know how sort-of needy she's been in the last couple of months. The more I think about it, the more I'm convinced there's something not quite right in that perfect marriage. She never goes with

Derek on his trips. When she gets back we'll have a girls' lunch and find out what's going on. Mind you, between you and me, I've never really liked Derek. He's too secretive and moody.

Yes, I've been drinking camomile tea at night as you suggested, and it has helped me sleep better. I've bought some soy milk too, and the linseed and soy mixture to sprinkle on my cereal. But your anti-anxiety pills don't seem to be working. I still feel worried and anxious most of the time.

Lucy, there's something I really have to say. I felt pretty angry when you said you thought I let James mould my life to suit himself. I am not some kind of jelly, although I do feel a bit wobbly being on my own after having a loving partner for so many years. He did not mould my life, he was just very good to me. He took care of everything and was faithful and kind and hard-working, and I don't like you criticising him now he's gone. And I'm not 'just at home vegetating', I'm making an effort to get out and about, as you well know. I'm not as flamboyant and feisty as you are, but nor do I want to be. That's you. I'm me.

Well, I've got that off my chest. I hope you don't mind me being honest. Must go and do my homework.

Love as always, Cath

February 17

ATTENTION: LUCY FINDLAY (PRIVATE AND CONFIDENTIAL)

Well, you certainly answered fast, and I'm so glad we've cleared all that up.

Thanks for asking about SPUDS. I must say that I do think this course will give me more confidence, just through teaching me new things and helping me meet people. A woman called Lani Trethowan takes us for computer classes and she's really good. Calm and patient, and only young, maybe thirty-five or so.

Marcus Candover, who takes basic psychology, is about our age and a real spunk, as Fe would put it. All the women in my class, except Pam and me, are besotted by him, but he seems oblivious to their charms. He's very good-looking, a bit like Robert Redford when he was younger.

I don't want anyone yet. It's far too soon. In fact, I'm not sure if I'll ever want a man in my life again. But if and when I do, I've decided it has to be someone either very rich or very practical.

I'm a bit concerned about taking testosterone. I hope I don't grow a moustache and hairy legs. When I was having my hair done the other day, a woman was getting waxed behind a screen and she was screaming her head off. I didn't scream when I had Amy or Fe, and waxing can't be worse than having a baby. Perhaps she was just one of those hairy, nervy women.

Have you had a bone-density test yet? Mine is 96 per cent, which they said is very good for my age. There's osteoporosis on my side of the family. You've seen Mum – she's stooped over like a fish-hook. I don't want to end up like her, all bent and shrivelled.

Speaking of shrivelled, Peg-down-the-road's doctor told her that a menopausal woman's womb shrivels to the size of a walnut. Surely that's not true? And if it is, why do our stomachs get bigger, not smaller? Lucky you, you don't seem to be suffering from any middle-age spread. Probably having your womb out helps. I just have to look at a cake and it morphs straight onto my hips.

Another thing I've noticed is that my lips are getting thinner. About the only part of my body that is! Have a look next time we have lunch and tell me honestly whether you think I should use lip-liner to make them look fuller, or whether that will make them look even more obvious.

Did I tell you that Fe's friend Alice is getting collagen injections in her lips? (You've met her I think. They call her Ali.) She's only twenty-five. She accidentally sent me an email meant for Fe. Alice's sex life would make your hair curl, and she'd be so embarrassed if she knew I'd read all about her new boyfriend IN DETAIL. He proposed to her on top of a ferris wheel, apparently, and now she's thinking she'd like to get married on top of a ferris wheel too, because it'd be romantic. I hope Fe never decides to get married on top of something. I can't cope with heights.

Next month Fe says she's going to something called the Festival of Kurban Bayrami. She tells me that people buy a sheep (if they can afford one) and slit its throat, and then have a feast. It's something to do with Abraham sacrificing a ram instead of his son, which sounds a bit gruesome. But then I suppose Fe should respect Turkish customs while she's there. It sounds like she's eating a lot of lamb, though everyone says too much meat isn't good for you.

Love as always, Cath

February 19

DEAR AMY

Lovely to hear that Sydney is crawling and has been promoted to Turtles. And can Dakota really count backwards from ten? I loved the story about him yelling, 'No smoking!'

at the council workers having a smoko in the car park. I'm sure they were very impressed.

Yes, I do miss the children and I wish I could come to Virginia and Georgia's callisthenics competition, but it's best not to travel until my hernia's fixed. I don't want it blowing up in the plane.

Love from your mother x

February 20

Dear Fe

I don't know when you'll get this, but I just thought I should mention osteoporosis again. Your grandma's seems to be getting worse. It runs in the family, and that's why you're supposed to drink lots of milk. Are you? There must be cows in Turkey, even in remote places, or do they drink goat's milk? I'm sure that would do the same job. Or even camel's milk. Don't forget to take those calcium tablets I put in your first-aid kit. They'll help your health generally, and your teeth and nails and hair as well as your bones.

I was pleased to get your last email. Ephesus sounds fascinating – all those Roman ruins. I looked it up on the Internet. Paul's letters to the Ephesians in the Bible, and all that. When I told Pam during basic psychology, she said loudly, so everyone could hear, 'Do you know what the Ephesians said when they got letter number thirty from Paul? "Not more junk mail!"' Then Marcus Candover, our tutor, discussed the psychology of junk mail, which was very interesting. Have I mentioned him before? He's gorgeous-looking, and all the females in the group except Pam (who's got a 'gentleman caller') and me (I still love your father) are going gaga over him. You've never seen so much exposed cleavage.

This is the first time you've really opened up to me about Dad dying and how it's affected you. Maybe seeing all those sunburnt British people riding around on scooters triggered it a bit, because your father always got sunburnt. When you said you felt like a part of you died with him – well, that's how I feel too. I put on a brave face for everyone, but inside I feel as if I've shrivelled up in my soul. I still forget, even though it's nearly a year now, and I set a place for him at the table and cook enough food for two, instead of one. I know this sounds silly, but sometimes I take his urn off the mantelpiece and put it on his chair, so he can be at the table with me. It makes me feel closer to him. But I guess I'll gradually learn to cope. Life goes on.

Thank you for the T-shirts. Unfortunately I've put

on more weight, so next time perhaps you could send a larger size. And maybe choose navy, or something in more muted tones. Not that I don't appreciate these ones, but it's a waste of money if I can't fit into them or the colour doesn't suit me. Anyway, I don't want you to spend all your money on me. Just a little spoon or something would do.

Make sure you eat lots of lentils, they're very good for you. And plenty of fruit.

Is Yasul a reliable kind of chap? Have you met his family? Does he have a job?

Love from Mum xx

February 21

Dear Amy

Yes, I was surprised too that Fe's email address is Fewee@hotmail.com. It does sound a bit, well, rude. Perhaps she was going to use 'WeeFe' (remember how your father used to call her that when she was little?), but it was already taken.

Personally I think it's good she's hooked up with Yasul, as you put it, because hopefully he'll look after her in those remote areas she keeps visiting. Fe has good judgement, even though you think she's just 'your hopeless little sister'. You should give her more credit.

Love from your mother x

February 21

ATTENTION: LUCY FINDLAY (PRIVATE AND CONFIDENTIAL)

I've been having the most horrendous hot flushes. I had one when I went to see the bank manager and he said, 'There's no need to be embarrassed about your financial situation, Mrs Morgan.' I told him I wasn't embarrassed, just menopausal, and he said, 'What's that got to do with your financial affairs?' I said, 'Nothing, but it's why I look red and flustered. It's my hormones. They're dwindling.' He said, 'So is your bank balance.' He wasn't at all interested in my symptoms.

There should be more menopausal bank managers, then they'd understand what we go through. His total lack of sympathy made me lose my train of thought and I couldn't remember what he'd told me. I think I need a financial adviser, one who speaks plain English. I heard you have to be careful, though, as some of them have a vested interest and push you into whatever suits them.

See you Thursday, after the op.

Love as always, Cath

February 22

Dear Fe

I'm sorry I sent my email to all your friends. But I'm sure they didn't really mind. In fact, they probably liked getting cheery news from home. And it's not as if I was discussing too many personal details, was I? I can't really remember. But yes, I do understand that I have to click on Reply, and not Reply All.

I'm looking forward to staying with Lucy for a couple of days after my operation. She's so good with all things medical. She's always been so calm and controlled around blood. Even when we were kids and she accidentally dropped a knife on my foot she didn't panic. You can never replace friends who go way back, even when your lives are quite different. She's got a career and is sales manager for Eternal Life and is into the New Age and spiritual journeys. Whereas I'm not! But it does mean she'll give me a lot of herbals while I'm staying with her. She says they'll help with my healing.

Speaking of journeys, I heard on talkback that some hostesses in Japan have sexual relationships with their clients. I hope Michelle wouldn't lower herself by doing such a thing. I'm glad you decided not to be a hostess. Email me soon, won't you?

Love from Mum xx

February 23

ATTENTION: LUCY FINDLAY (PRIVATE AND CONFIDENTIAL)

Oh my God, I just got the most horrendous email from Fe. She's in jail! Well, it said Jails, so maybe it's a prison complex? I don't know why she's there, but I know she'd never do anything criminal.

I realise this is a big ask, but could you possibly drop Darwin and fly to Turkey with me? This is an emergency! I tried phoning your mobile but there was no answer. I'm terribly worried. Please answer ASAP.

Cath

February 23

DEAR AMY

I'm glad I caught you on the phone. I took your advice and rang the Turkish consulate, but no one's answering. I can't say I think you're very sympathetic. And I *certainly* don't agree that Fe's safer in jail than wandering through the Middle East. Jails in other countries are atrocious. I don't think they even have sanitation, let alone proper meals.

Maybe saying that is your way of trying to comfort me. Well, it's not comforting at all! I'm going to Turkey on my own if no one will go with me. Please don't tell Grandma and Grandpa, as they'll only worry.

Your very worried mother

February 23

Dear Ambassador

Are you there? No one is answering your phone. Can you please check the Orange Pension Jails in Turkey and find out which one is holding my daughter, Fiona Catherine Morgan. And on what charges? Please phone or email me immediately.

Thank you.

Catherine Morgan

February 23

Dear Amy

I know you can't drop everything and go to Turkey, but could you at least try to help me find out where Fe is? I've phoned everyone there I can think of – the embassy, the police, even the hospitals in case she was injured. I am frantic.

Your mother

February 23

Attention: Lucy Findlay (Private and Confidential)

You are the best friend ever! Thank you, thank you for arranging to come with me, *and* for giving up your frequent flyer points to get the air tickets. Yes, I'll be ready to leave tomorrow. I'll bind my tummy with my long blue silk scarf so that if my hernia explodes it will be contained.

Love as always, Cath

February 23

Attention: Lucy Findlay (Private and Confidential)

I tried to phone you on your mobile but you're out of range. Wonderful news! I just heard from Fe. She rang me because someone at the Australian embassy in Istanbul phoned her, after Dwayne rang the American embassy there. She's not in jail, it was just a typo. She meant *Jamil's* – it's a pension and Jamil is a person.

I feel so stupid for panicking, but if Rohan emailed you and said he was in jail, you'd panic too. Anyway, Fe's safe. The place she's staying at is in the middle of some orange groves and that's why it's called the Orange Pension. She's met this chap Jamil whose cousin owns the pension, and he's going to take her to meet his family.

It seems they live in the middle of nowhere near some underground caves – or in some underground caves, I'm not sure. It all sounds far too dangerous to me, as it's near Kurd country and there are bandits in the hills.

Part of me still wants to go over there immediately, but Fe would be so angry. She says I don't trust her at all. And I feel stupid enough as it is about all this. I don't know what's happened to the backpacker friends she was with, they seem to have disappeared into thin air. And she seems to be drinking litres of beer and raki – that's the local drink, made of aniseed apparently. It can't be good for her – women can't cope with alcohol as well as men because of their hormones, and raki sounds very potent. I just wish she'd find herself in a hurry and come home.

Your constantly worried friend Cath

February 24

Dear Fe

I know I jumped to a silly conclusion. It was all my fault and I'm sorry I embarrassed you. I'm just glad you're safe. Thanks so much for calling to let me know.

Thanks for understanding about the T-shirts too, and

yes, I'll send the one with the donkey on it to Aunt Helene on your behalf. It was nice of you to think of her, seeing she never worries about our side of the family. Not that Uncle Robert does either, really. He'd like Grandma and Grandpa to go into a nursing home, but why should they when they're happy at home? Who knows how long we'll have them? None of my friends still have their parents.

Mind you, I could do with a bit more help, though I'd never let them know that. It can be tiring cooking extra meals and then delivering them, though of course I do enjoy the visits. I know you think they should get Meals on Wheels, but Grandpa doesn't like the food. He phoned them up last time and told them, 'Friday's fish was off and today's steak was tough as old boots, so don't bother coming back.' He's not afraid to say what he thinks.

Aunt Helene and Uncle Robert could do more to help, but I think they think that once it gets too hard for me I'll give in and convince your grandparents to go into a home. Of course, it's that big block of land in a prime position that's the attraction. Robert wants to bulldoze their house and put up units. Over my dead body! Not that I'm against nursing homes, but your grandparents can still manage at home, with some help. And I don't believe in bulldozing lovely old houses to put up hideous apartments. Your grandpa would come back and haunt them. He's always saying things like, 'Soon the whole bloody planet will be covered in concrete.' If he knew what Uncle Robert had in mind, he'd have a heart attack.

Yes, I certainly still miss your father. He was such an anchor, even though he never really talked all that much – he mostly just watched TV. But he was there, if you know what I mean. The hardest part is having to do those little jobs around the house. But I'm getting quite good at them. I climbed up on the roof to adjust the TV aerial the other day, even though I'm terrified of heights.

I know you're missing him too, Fe, but he wouldn't want you to be unhappy about him. He'd want you to get on with your life and enjoy yourself. I know you feel sad that he didn't live to see you get your marketing degree, but I also know he'd be very proud of you.

Yes, my operation has been rescheduled. It's next week now. But don't worry, I'll be in good hands.

I hope you're well. Take care.

Love from Mum xx

February 25

ATTENTION: LUCY FINDLAY (PRIVATE AND CONFIDENTIAL)

Have you heard from Jane? She sent me a postcard of pigeons in Trafalgar Square, but all she said was, 'Having a lovely time. Love, Jane.' No return address, so I can't write to her.

Do you think she'll get time to pop in and see Barry and Rohan? Did you give her Barry's address? I mean, it's not like Barry wouldn't want to see her, is it? After all, we were your bridesmaids when you two got married, and of course she was at Rohan's christening too. Though she might feel odd that she hasn't seen either of them since you and Barry split up. Anyway, perhaps you could phone Barry and ask him if he's heard from her, so at least then we'll know if she's all right. Or not. I am fed up with not knowing if people overseas are all right or lying dead under a bridge.

I hope my operation goes ahead next week. I'll be in a real fix if it's postponed, since you're interstate the week after. I wish hospitals would get better organised, but I suppose they do have to deal with emergencies and not just hernias.

Love as always, Cath x

February 26

Dear Fe

Your sister told me she received your email, but she didn't appreciate your joke about her getting pregnant at Disneyland and calling the next child Disney. I know Marla conceived the girls in Virginia and Georgia, but it was Dwayne who wanted to keep the tradition going when Amy got pregnant in Dakota and Sydney. (That reminds me of when she thought Dakota was going to be twins and you said she'd have to call them North Dakota and South Dakota. Now that *was* quite funny.)

Anyway, I'm probably not supposed to tell you this, but she won't be getting pregnant any more because Dwayne's had his tubes cut.

I do love getting the email photos. I was very relieved to hear that Jamil's family don't live in underground caves.

Love from Mum xx

February 26

Dear Amy

Thanks for your offer of a home in Sydney yet again, but we've discussed all this before and I still want to stay here. I know my house is old and needs repair, I know I have some money hassles and I know you've repeatedly offered to look after me, but I don't want to move to Sydney and live with you and help look after Dakota and Sydney.

I mean, I love them both, so don't think I don't want to be with them. And I do know how expensive day care and after-school care are, and that you and Dwayne have to work to make ends meet. And I do understand that a blended family is hard. It's understandable, too, that the girls want to fly to the States to see their mother, but she did relinquish custody to pursue her acting career. And she doesn't seem that interested in them, apart from the occasional phone call. It's quite sad, really.

Anyway, I get lonely sometimes but my life is here, with my friends, and I need to look after Grandma and Grandpa. So while it's very kind of you, I'm still saying no.

The other news at this end is brief. I'm still in SPUDS. I'm really enjoying psychology with Marcus Candover, not just because he's so easy to look at, but because I'm learning so much about feelings. I still have to deal with scattering your father's ashes. Marcus says I need closure. I can't bring myself to do it, but I know your father can't stay on the mantelpiece for ever.

Remember I'll be at Lucy's place next week.

Love from your mother xx

February 27

Attention: Lucy Findlay (Private and Confidential)

It was great catching up for lunch the other day. Darwin sounded wonderful. And I knew you'd like Pam. You seemed very interested in her 'gentleman caller'. She says he's 'clean and kind' and doesn't pressure her. He visits her once a week, pampers her and they have sex, and that's it.

But don't you think it's odd that she doesn't want to know anything about his life? He's told her his wife is an invalid and they can't have a sexual relationship, and she prefers him to be a gentleman caller rather than go to a brothel. Do you think that's true? At least it allows Pam to do what she's doing with a clear conscience, I suppose, although curiosity would get the better of me. I'd want to know where he lives so I could drive past and check out the house, and see what his wife looks like.

In a way, though, it might be better to have a married lover than to fall in love with someone different every fifteen minutes, like you seem to, and then having dramas and getting emotionally devastated. I must say it was very embarrassing when Pam started talking about sexually transmitted diseases at the top of her voice and the whole cafe turned to look at us. I'd never even thought about women our age getting an STD; it would be so humiliating to have to go to the doctor.

I wonder where a woman could find a clean, kind gentleman caller? Not that I want one, of course. It wouldn't be fair to James's memory, and anyway I think I'd have to be in love with someone before I could have a sexual relationship with him.

Amy and Dwayne are still nagging me to live with them, but all that means is they'd get a cheap babysitter and I'd lose out. I have my friends around me here, and if I went to live in Sydney who'd look after my parents?

Must dash, I have to go to the dentist about this tooth that's been annoying me. I hope it isn't another abscess. Mum says that teeth are a problem from the minute you're born till the minute you die. I think my gums must be shrinking and exposing the nerves, because all my teeth ache at times. Isn't it ironic that my lips and gums are the only parts of my body that are shrinking? Everything else is expanding. I look like the Michelin man. Maybe I'll look thinner when my hernia's done?

Love as always, Cath

P.S. Haven't heard from Jane since that postcard I told you about. She must be putting all her energies into nurturing her marriage. I agree with your intuition – there's something she's not telling us.

February 27

DEAR FE

Thanks for your email and more photos. The Valley of the Fairy Chimneys looks lovely, all those little pink cones with dark tops. Are they volcanoes? I just had a tooth filled, so my mouth feels rather like a dormant volcano. The walk through the valley with all those nesting pigeons sounds very picturesque, but the smell must have been dreadful. And I don't like the idea of you sleeping on a hillside, even if it did mean you got to see the sun rise on those old stone heads. You could have been robbed or murdered by a rebel Kurd, despite the fact that Jamil was with you.

What a shame he has to stay behind to look after his family's goats and apricots, and can't go with you to Syria. But you say you've met someone called Raji – who is he, besides being an Indian living in Turkey? I think it's safer to travel in a group, really.

Love from Mum xx

February 28

ATTENTION: LUCY FINDLAY (PRIVATE AND CONFIDENTIAL)

There's no need to get huffy because I said you fall in love every fifteen minutes. It was just a figure of speech. But be honest, you *do* seem to rather frequently . . .

Fe has been in some remote part of Turkey, sleeping on the side of a hill with Jamil. To her it's all a big adventure, but to me it's just plain foolish. Jamil's apparently gone back to his family's farm, but she's going to Syria with an Indian man called Raji. She met him when his donkey trod on her foot. Syria doesn't have emails, she says.

I'm trying to be calm. But what will she do next?

Love as always, Cath

February 29

LUCY FINDLAY (PRIVATE AND CONFIDENTIAL)

More hassles. Dad's got pleurisy, which apparently could turn into pneumonia. I feel guilty because I think it's my fault. I took him to the beach the other day and it turned quite cold and windy. One of those southerly busters just blew in from nowhere. I should have made him stay in the car, but he wanted to walk on the pier. You know how stubborn he can be, even though he's really quite frail. He held onto the railing and shambled right to the end and back. There were men fishing, and people walking and chatting in other languages. Of course, Dad said in a loud voice, 'This pier is full of wogs.' Luckily he didn't have his teeth in and I don't think anyone could understand him.

I really must get Fe to cut down on her spending. She seems to think I'm a money tree. She's told me she'd bought five big copper trays and sent them home by airmail, so she needs more money. At least the hostels she stays in are only ten dollars a night and the food is cheap, but she'll have to stop buying things until I know what my financial situation is. I just hope the muddle James left gets sorted out soon.

I wish I could stop worrying about Fe and Mum and Dad, and just get on with my own life. Meanwhile I must go and weed the garden. The thistles are up to my waist near the back fence.

Love as always, Cath

P.S. Still no word from Jane. I saw a movie on TV the other night where a man took his wife overseas, then murdered her and dumped her body in a garbage bin. How would we ever know if Derek did that to Jane?

March 1

DEAR FE

Thank you for sending me your itinerary for the next two weeks. Now I know I can find you if I have to, and also where you are if you disappear.

I've enrolled in a handywoman class. I need to learn some skills so I can do repairs at home. I think it's time I got a part-time job or something, for the income, though I'm not sure what I can do. After all, I haven't worked since I got married. It won't be office work, because as you know I'm still a two-finger typist. Maybe I could work in a shop a few days a week.

Do take care of yourself.

Love from Mum xx

March 1

DEAR AMY

This will be brief, as you reminded me that your workplace doesn't approve of 'email clutter' on your computer. Thanks for offering to pay my airfare up for Virginia's birthday, but I have enough fly-buys for a ticket. I'll phone you later in the week from Lucy's house, when I'm convalescing.

Love from your mother x

March 8

Dear Fe

Yes, I know Lucy emailed you to say the operation went smoothly, and it did. I'm home now. Lucy looked after me very well.

So you're still in Turkey with Raji – I thought you were going to get a bus across the border to Syria? I'm glad to hear you've cut down on Turkish beer and are drinking more tea.

But Fe, I'm afraid you'll have to cut down on your spending too, because I'm starting to run out of money. Bob Lancaster, the accountant who took care of Dad's business affairs, came to visit me and explained that he's still sorting things out even though probate has been granted. He said there should be more money and he's not sure where it is. It seems he and your father were in some business deals together. I'm sure Bob is trustworthy, he's such a nice man. I'd never met him before – he took over old Henry Sims' firm when Henry retired.

I'm trying to understand the portfolios and trusts and things your father set up for his retirement. Anyway, Bob has offered to manage the investments for me and also track down the missing money. He's such a kind man.

I'm really enjoying the psychology sessions at SPUDS,

although I had to miss this week's. Pam thinks I'm the teacher's pet because Marcus Candover seems to pay more attention to me than anyone else, though they're all still throwing themselves at him. Last week we learnt the broken-record technique, which you're supposed to use on tradesmen and shop assistants who won't refund your money. You don't get into an argument or get emotionally sidetracked, you just keep repeating the same simple statement over and over. We did a role-play and I did quite well. A bossy man in my class was the shop assistant and he was really aggressive, but I stood my ground and kept repeating, 'I want my money back, please,' and he eventually gave in.

I've already tried this technique on your grandfather. When he refused to have a bath I just kept saying, 'You're having a bath,' over and over, and in the end he did. I must try it on Uncle Robert: 'Visit your parents. Visit your parents.' You could try it too if you get stuck in any difficult situations, and let me know if it works. 'Get your hands off me! Get your hands off me!' Just keep repeating it.

Speaking of hands, I had my first handywoman class last week and we learnt to use power tools. Next week it's little plumbing jobs, like replacing washers. The doctor said that as long as I don't lift anything heavy I'll be okay. There are ten women in the class. Most of them are on their own, widowed or divorced. One had a husband who suddenly took himself off to India to join an ashram, leaving her with a bunch of leaky taps, so she wants to know about plumbing. Her name's Gaye and I think we'll be friends.

I'm also trying to read some uplifting books, now that I can read in bed without annoying your father – and now that I have more time to read. I've just finished *The Fascinating History of Your Lunch*. It's about civilisations and their food.

Do watch what you eat in Turkey. Wash the fruit. And the vegies. In fact, you should only eat them well cooked. Do you want me to send some ointment for your bruised foot?

Love from Mum xx

March 9

ATTENTION: LUCY FINDLAY (PRIVATE AND CONFIDENTIAL)

Yes, it worked in very well, didn't it, you being home the week after my op. And now I'm recuperating and you're in Brisbane. We were lucky there!

I hope Fe doesn't get gangrene. As you know, a donkey trod on her foot. She says it's recovering, but how can I be sure? Oh, speaking of feet, I heard this joke on the radio: Did you hear about the guy who decided he wanted an unusual pet? He bought a centipede in a little white box. Once he was home he decided to take his new pet out for a drink. So he asked the centipede, 'Would you like to come to the pub with me and have a beer?' No answer. He waited a few minutes and then asked again, 'How about going to the pub for a drink?' Still no answer. So he decided to try one more time, and put his face right up against the centipede's box and shouted, 'Hey, in there! Would you like to go to the pub and have a beer?' A little voice came out of the box. 'I heard you the first time! I'm just putting on my shoes.'

Speaking of shoes, I wonder if Jane has done much shopping in London. I know she wanted to buy shoes. I must say I'm getting more and more worried. I got another postcard, this time from Buckingham Palace, and it also said 'Having a lovely time. Love, Jane.' It's a bit odd, don't you think?

Love as always, Cath

P.S. I've stopped taking the anti-anxiety pills. They weren't working and they made me feel woozy. Dr Valushi is increasing my hormone doses: Trieste 12, progesterone 200, testosterone 7.5, DHEA 5. And she's deleted the memory one, as it was very expensive and not doing anything much, really.

March 12

Dear Fe

I don't know what happened – I emailed you a few days ago. How could it have just disappeared? Anyway, thanks for calling, and here's another one. It's a bit hard to type at the moment, as my shoulder is aching. I think it's an old injury. I should have had it looked at when I got my hernia done. I hope it won't need an operation. But if it does, I might wait until something else falls off or collapses and see if I can get a package deal.

It didn't help my shoulder heaving three bags of horse manure out of the shed yesterday and shovelling it onto the garden. But someone has to do it. I know I'm not allowed to lift things yet, but I didn't exactly lift the bags, I dragged them. I can hear you saying, Mum, you shouldn't be hauling manure. But what am I supposed to do? What with your sister in Sydney and you in the Middle East. But I thank God for my two healthy daughters, even if they are both far away. I can manage.

I'm thinking of going to Grey Power weight-resistance classes for over-fifties. There's no heavy lifting involved, of course, but weight resistance is supposed to prevent osteoporosis and all sorts of ailments.

It'll be good to exercise my stomach muscles. When

I was your age I used to look at fat middle-aged stomachs and think, What the hell is in there? Now I have a fat stomach myself and I honestly don't know why. I'm not eating much. It must be loose muscles.

I'm sorry to keep harping, Fe, but you really must try to not spend so much. Maybe don't buy any more souvenirs or presents just yet.

I met with Bob the accountant to go over the finances. I gave him all your father's paperwork, and he didn't know anything about the foreign bank account I found. He says we may never know what happened to all the money. It could have been invested in bad shares and lost, for all I know. Anyway, since Bob invested money along with your father in these deals, he naturally wants to get it back. And my money too, of course.

Bob and I had a sandwich lunch at that little place near the mall. He's a nice man and always treats me with good old-fashioned courtesy. Did you know that Lord Sandwich invented the sandwich?

Love from Mum xx

March 13

DEAR VIRGINIA

Fancy me getting an email from you at school on Grandparents Day. What a good idea. I know you're not allowed to visit chat rooms on your father's computer, but maybe if you asked nicely he might let you email me sometimes.

Yes, Harriet is wagging her tail and Henry is cleaning his whiskers. One day your mother and father might allow you to have a pet, although I think you'd have more hope of getting a kitten than a baby Vietnamese pig, even if they are cute. Email me again when you can, and Georgia too.

I'll see you on your birthday.

Love from Grandma Morgan xx

March 15

DEAR FE

I think today is The Odes of March. Where are you? I haven't heard from you for a while.

Love from Mum xx

March 16

Dear Fe

Are you all right? Are you receiving my emails? Have you reached Viagra Pension yet?

March 18

Dear Amazing Penile Growth

No, I am not interested in purchasing Viagra, thank you.

Sincerely, Catherine Morgan

March 19

Dear Fe

Thank God you're all right, though your email was brief. Did you *really* think Raji's family were offering you turds for dinner when it was curds? Curds and whey are sort of like yoghurt – which reminds me, you should eat lots of curds, for the calcium.

Sandra Wisenbone next door wants me to talk at a women's expo thing on Tuesday, about my experience with plant hormones. The expo's about women's health and rights and money. I'm on a panel called Menopause and You.

No, I am not falling for Marcus Candover. Anyway,

he's far too sophisticated and polished to be interested in me. And I'm too busy with the handywoman course. Plus I'm about to start the weight-resistance classes with Pam, twice a week for an hour. I had an interview with the head instructor. He said to go gently at first, due to the op, and gradually work up to heavier weights.

So I have plenty to occupy myself with at the moment. This week I'm flying up to Sydney for Virginia's birthday party. I'll arrive on Friday night, the party's on Saturday, then I'll fly back on Sunday afternoon. A nice little break. Lucy will pop in and feed Harriet and Henry, and water the garden.

Love from Mum xx

March 19

ATTENTION: LUCY FINDLAY (PRIVATE AND CONFIDENTIAL)

I've been getting harassing emails offering me Viagra and vibrators and heaven knows what. One said 'Click here' if I wanted to be deleted from their mailing list, but when I did, more emails came – for stuff called Cucumber Comfort and Dynamic Dolphin. I think that's disgusting! Imagine if a child got hold of it. Pam says I should get another email address and that'll stop the harassment.

Love as always, Cath

P.S. Did you get a postcard from Jane in France? Mine said the same thing again: 'Having a lovely time. Love, Jane.' In that movie I told you about, the husband made his wife write postcards before he killed her, and then he posted them from different countries so her family would think she was alive. What should we do?

March 20

Dear Fe

I'm sorry you broke up with Raji, but as I keep telling you, you get involved too soon. Why should a man want to marry you when he gets it all free? Look at your friend Alice: if she can get a decent proposal from a decent man, so can you. Amy got married when she was twenty-four and she said it was the perfect age. Don't leave it too late. As you get older it gets more difficult to have babies because your pelvic floor and hips are more rigid.

Then again, maybe you should forget about men while you're overseas. You'd probably find a nicer man back here. Supermarkets are good places to look. I found your father at the supermarket, near the personal-hygiene section (I was buying deodorant and he was buying shaving cream).

I know you don't like me to talk about your private life, so I won't mention it again after this. I just want to say don't jump into bed with men so early in the relationship. I know it's fashionable, but men aren't like women. They have an uncontrollable need for sex at times. Keep well. I'll be at Amy's if you need me.

Love from Mum xx

March 20

DEAR AMY

Yes, I arrive at seven tomorrow night. Will you meet me at the airport or will I catch a cab?

Love from your mother

P.S. Please note my new email address: cathmo55@bigpond.com – due to me getting pornographic emails about vibrators.

March 20

LUCY FINDLAY (PRIVATE AND CONFIDENTIAL)

What do you mean, buy a dolphin? I don't think it's funny at all! Also, it's denigrating dolphins. Lucy, if you want one of those stupid gadgets, go ahead and buy one, but

I don't want to know about it. Call me a prude, but . . . Enough.

I'm going to Sydney tomorrow, so I probably won't email you till I get back. And anyway you'll be in London. I know you can't stop off in the Middle East to check on Fe, but can you at least check on Jane? Did you see on the news where the body of a woman was found in a rubbish skip in Sydney? The police say there are suspicious circumstances. Aren't you worried?

Love as always, Cath

March 26

DEAR AMY

Thank you so much for the mini-holiday. I really enjoyed Virginia's birthday party. I'm sorry I couldn't stay on until Easter, but I'm needed here. Grandpa had a small accident with the TV, so it was just as well I came back when I did.

Love from your mother x

March 27

Dear Fe

I had a lovely time in Sydney. Dwayne borrowed a digital video camera from work to film Virginia's party for Marla and her husband. He said he'd email you a copy.

Virginia had thirty little friends for a theme party and they all came dressed as a Barbie. Virginia wore pink – she was Fairy Barbie – and Georgia wore leopard skin for Jungle Barbie. Dakota wanted to be a Barbie too! They dressed him in an old aqua nappy and told him he was Water Barbie. Sydney wasn't dressed as anything, except himself.

Amy and Dwayne hired a jumping castle and a clown, and had it catered by Kidz Parties Inc. in a striped marquee. You should have seen Virginia doing her jazz ballet and the splits in the jumping castle. I wish your father had been there to see it.

Kidz Parties did a good job, I suppose, but really, Amy could have done just as well. It was only sausage rolls and party pies, those little sausages on sticks, and fairy bread. But Amy says everyone gets outsiders to cater for their kids' parties. Apparently it's quite competitive. I don't agree with hiring all that stuff and having a party catered for when it's only a tenth birthday. It must have cost a fortune. Amy said Dwayne put it on Visa to get the fly-buy points for America – he'll be paid for by the company, of course, but the rest of the family won't.

You'd be surprised how much the children have grown since you've been away. You're missing all Dakota's sayings and doings and Sydney's gurglings. He says 'Cha cha, cha cha' all the time, so his nickname is Cha-Cha. Maybe you should ring your sister and then you could listen to him over the phone? Amy would love to hear from you. I don't think a phone call to Sydney costs more than one to Melbourne. And Dakota is so gorgeous. He keeps saying, 'When's my Auntie Flea coming to stay? I miss Auntie Flea'.

I babysat on Saturday night while Amy and Dwayne went to dinner with friends. Sydney was good, and went straight to sleep after I sang him fifteen songs. The girls and Dakota weren't interested in playing Snakes and Ladders or Monopoly or Old Maid, like Amy said. After Dakota went to sleep, Virginia and Georgia wanted to watch a DVD they'd borrowed from a friend. I didn't think it was suitable, it was all about ghosts and goblins, but they said they're allowed to watch horror movies. Dwayne says they know the difference between reality and imagination.

The next day everyone was tried and cranky. The children hadn't had enough sleep. I think Dwayne was hung-over. In the afternoon we caught the ferry to Manly and the children had a swim. Dwayne and Amy seemed to be having a tiff, something about a woman called Leonie. But it was really none of my business.

Let me know when you get to Aleppo. You should be able to get the money there – I put it in your account yesterday. But go easy, Bob hasn't sorted everything out yet.

Love from Mum xx

March 27

ATTENTION: LUCY FINDLAY (PRIVATE AND CONFIDENTIAL)

No, I didn't not email because I was cross with you for thinking the vibrator stuff was funny. And I haven't been sulking, I was in Sydney. I'm sure I told you I was staying the weekend.

Yes, Dad's much better, thanks. But Mum's developed an ulcer on her heel. It's too painful for her to walk, and as you know she has trouble walking anyway, even without an ulcerated heel. And yes, I've heard from Fe, and while I'm not happy about her rambling all over the Middle East with strange men, I have to grin and bear it.

Fancy Bob Lancaster being on the same plane and sitting next to you! It's a small world, isn't it? I knew he was going to London for a week or so, but I didn't know he was going to Europe. I guess he has business over there. A pity he slept most of the way. I'm sure you'd like him.

I desperately hope you find Jane. If she hasn't been to see Barry and Rohan, and she and Derek have checked out of the hotel they were at, I wonder where she is. It's the Consolidated Merchant Bank that Derek works for – they must know where he's staying. Do you think it's too early to contact the police?

I'm sorry if I offended you with my comments about the Dynamic Dolphin. I guess I am a bit prudish, but I haven't really been exposed to all that stuff. Not that I'm saying you have, but I know you're more experimental than I am in those areas. You don't mind having one-night stands because they might turn into long-term relationships, whereas I don't think I could. I'd feel bad. And I don't like the idea of being hopeless at modern-day sex with a stranger.

Fe seems to be flitting from one man to another. I know you're going to laugh and say that's normal at her age. But I don't want her to end up like Peg-down-the-road's cousin's daughter Melissa, who's had five children to five different men. Peg says she's only doing it to get the welfare payments, but who'd want to make a career out of having children for money? There's no way Fe's anything like Melissa, so I should trust her not to do something foolish. Pam thinks that Fe might be looking for a substitute father figure.

Love as always, Cath

March 29

ATTENTION: LUCY FINDLAY (PRIVATE AND CONFIDENTIAL)

Sorry to keep going on about my family, but I do worry about the way Amy and Dwayne are bringing up the children. They seem to me to be over-scheduled. So many classes, and not one day free after school to just be themselves and play.

You know, when I asked Dwayne about Virginia and Georgia watching horror movies, he said, 'Censorship isn't necessary. We trust the girls to be discriminating.' Whatever that means. When I told Amy the movie was full of gore, she said, 'Try watching the nightly news on TV. That's reality horror.' I think they believe that because the friend who lent them the DVD has a father who's a lawyer and a mother who's a psychiatrist, and they're pillars of Sydney's social set, whatever the friend does is okay. It's a strange values system, if you ask me, and not at all like the way James and I brought up our kids.

Of course, it's difficult with the girls because they're not Amy's flesh and blood. A couple of times I heard them say to her, 'You're not our real mother, we can do what we like.' But then I did warn her before she married Dwayne it'd be tough. I think she was swept off her feet by him because he was older, charming, sophisticated and American. She'd only really had one boyfriend since high school, and personally I don't think that's enough experience with men to make the best decision.

Not that Dwayne is the wrong decision – he's very nice and a good provider – but taking on a man with two kids when she was only twenty-four was a big responsibility. She does a good job, but Dwayne should make the girls treat her with more respect.

No, I haven't met any eligible men lately and I'm not looking for any, really. I'm still a grieving widow, even if you think I should get out more. You asked what I think of Bob: well, he's divorced, and divorced men often have more baggage than an airport carousel. Emotional baggage, I mean. Though Bob appears to be relatively uncluttered. Before he left he asked me what kind of perfume I liked, and when I said it was too expensive he said, 'You need spoiling, my dear.' Wasn't that sweet of him?

I was surprised the Consolidated Merchant Bank

refused to give you Derek's address and phone number because you're not kin, but I guess they have to be discreet. I wasn't actually suggesting you hang round the bank door in the hope of running into him, but surely there must be some way to find Jane?

Anyway, I hope you have a nice Easter in London. Don't eat too many chocolate eggs or get tangled up with needy men. Amy wanted me to go away with them at Easter, but I told her I preferred to stay home. They're hiring an on-site van on the central coast, and I would have had to sleep in the annexe with the girls, which wouldn't have been very restful.

And of course there's Mum and Dad. While I was in Sydney, Dad nearly electrocuted himself trying to fix the horizontal hold on the TV with a screwdriver. So I can't leave them again, and I can't ask Robert and Helene to come and look after them because they'd immediately see that it's a struggle for Mum and Dad to cope, which would advance the case for a nursing home.

In fact, I'm starting to change my mind about wanting Robert and Helene to help at all. They're better off out of it. But then it's all left to me, and that's not fair, is it? Not that I'm complaining, it's just that it's such a drama if I want to go away.

On a brighter note, we're going to learn how to build a dick in handywoman class. I'd like to have one right outside the French windows.

Love as always, Cath

March 29

ATTENTION: LUCY FINDLAY (PRIVATE AND CONFIDENTIAL)

It was a typo. I meant DECK!

April 2

DEAR FE

Wherever you are, Happy Easter! I'm sorry I can't give you a big hug and an Easter egg, but I'm thinking of you, far away near the land where it all started.

Dwayne told me that when he said to Dakota this morning that someone round and cuddly with soft hair came and left some little presents while he was asleep, Dakota yelled, 'Grandma!' Maybe I could hire myself out as the Easter Bunny?

Love from Mum xx

April 7

DEAR AMY

I'm glad you all had a lovely mini-break on the coast. It's a shame the weather was so terrible. The wind must have been incredibly strong to blow the annexe off the side of the van. You'd think they'd have attached it properly, wouldn't you? And a gum tree falling on the car! How fortunate you were all in the manager's office when it happened. It can't have been much fun driving home with all six of you squashed into a tiny Daewoo, but never mind, these things happen. The main thing is that you're all back home again, unscathed. I'm sure Dwayne will be able to do a good deal with the insurance company about the new car.

Have you heard from Fe lately? She's in Syria, in Aleppo, but she had trouble finding an Internet place over there. She had to go down some grotty alley to use a computer. Fortunately she met Ahmet, an up-to-date Turk who's in Syria on business, and he knew where this Internet place was.

Thanks for phoning Grandma and Grandpa for Easter. I'm sorry your grandfather called Dwayne 'a right-wing bloody idiot'. He probably thought it was the prime minister, though I guess Dwayne does vote right-wing. Your grandpa is always hopeful of getting a call from the prime minister because, as you know, he phones Parliament House every week or so to complain about something. We're not sure who answers the phone, but Grandpa is convinced it's the PM himself.

The latest thing to annoy Grandpa is the new laws they're planning to introduce for eighty-year-old motorists. He phoned last week to say they were discriminatory. He reckons it's not the old folk who cause accidents, but P-platers doing 100k in a 60k zone. He said, 'Have you ever seen an eighty-year-old doing donuts and wheelies down the main street?' I thought he had a good point there. Mind you, he's beyond driving a car himself nowadays.

Hugs and kisses for the children, and for yourself.

Love from your mother xx

April 7

Dear Fe

Thanks for your call the other night. It's good you're going to Damascus with some backpackers from the hostel. I feel much happier when you're travelling with a group.

I haven't really gone crazy because I talk to your father's urn, you know. Lucy says it's all part of the healing process.

'Just go with your feelings,' she says, 'and talk to him if you want to. Let him watch TV, especially the shows he used to love.' So do I.

I've already learnt to do small jobs like fix leaking taps and toilet cisterns in handywoman class, and have made friends with Gaye, the one who loves plumbing. Her husband found another woman in the ashram, as well as finding himself. Gaye's accepted it, and is happy to give him a divorce. He's prepared to let her keep the house and car, but apparently he needs their savings because he had to pay a large fee to join the ashram.

Must go. Hope all is well with you.

Love from Mum xx

April 9

ATTENTION: LUCY FINDLAY (PRIVATE AND CONFIDENTIAL)

I'm still trying to get over Jane – plastic surgery! And liposuction. Wouldn't you think she'd have told us? Her best friends? I could do with some plastic surgery myself, to get rid of my worry lines.

I can't believe she's been so selfish. Here we are worrying our heads off that Derek's murdered her, while all the time she's in a swish London hospital. Well, this plastic surgery had better be worth the effort, that's all I can say. But I guess since she was still wearing a compression stocking and had a bandaged face when you saw her, we won't know till she comes home.

I agree with you – why such an extreme makeover? Fat sucked out, breasts, nose and eyes done, chin tuck, tummy tuck – I can't believe she'd bother. It's not as if she's an actress, or someone famous. And it must've cost a fortune, though of course she had that money her aunt left her. I wonder how she was intending to explain her new look when she saw us?

I'm very happy she's okay, of course, but I could kill her for all the stress she's given me. When I told Mum and Dad, Mum said, 'I hope she hasn't got those coat-hanger eyebrows that make you look permanently surprised,' and Dad said, 'And a mouth like a Murray cod swimming upstream.'

On a happier note, I'm glad you got to spend some mother–son time with Rohan. I know you miss him, though at the time you did seem happy enough for him to go and live in London with Barry, just as you were about Tibby going to New York to be a model. I always thought it was very unselfish of you.

Speaking of children, I know you don't understand

why I worry so much about Fe. You see her as some sort of free spirit floating around getting her life together, whereas I think she's acting recklessly and getting her life in a mess. And she's so stubborn. I've told her again and again to keep to the tourist places, but she has to go wafting off to look at excavations in the middle of nowhere. Apparently there's a lot of digging going on in Syria. From her photos it looks like the surface of the moon. Now she's off to Damascus, but I wish she'd just come home.

Love as always, Cath

April 10

Dear Fe

I'm glad you were able to use the Internet in Damascus. It's fascinating to think that all those lovely stone buildings with their little rows of shops were there way back in the fifteenth century. They look so colourful and quaint in your photos.

How horrible, falling flat on your face in the street and being pinned down by your backpack. It was lucky Sven came along and helped you up. He looks like a nice chap – nicely cut blond hair and quite well dressed. Swedish, is he?

Yesterday I felt strong, so I pulled up the hall carpet. I thought I might as well use some of my handywoman skills. I did it in little sections so I wouldn't strain myself. Halfway through I got so tired I sat on the floor and cried. Then I got going again, and eventually I did it. Gaye says she'll help me put in the deck when I come to do it, and she's thinking of joining weight-resistance classes with Pam and me. She says that doing yoga and pilates has stretched her, but she needs to get stronger. That's where we handywomen fall down – we can't lug planks and lift heavy things. But we're finding we're good at the workmanship, especially attention to detail.

I just remembered you asked me what Gaye looks like: she's taller than me, and slim, except she has a podgy tummy from three Caesareans, and she's got blue eyes and shoulder-length brown hair. She's a bit older than me.

No, I'm not lonely, although I do miss you very much of course. Last night Bob Lancaster came to see me. He's back from Europe, where he managed to find the mystery (Swiss!) bank account, though there was only a hundred dollars in it. Anyway, he gave me advice on improving my financial situation and said he'd lend me some money at a very low interest rate, out of respect for your father. I might take him up on the offer.

I made a nice roast lamb with roasted potatoes and pumpkin and fresh green peas, and we had apple-and-rhubarb crumble for dessert. Bob spent a lot of time explaining stocks and shares and bulls and bears, but it's hard to follow. I wish I was better at maths.

Love from Mum xx

April 12

Dear Fe

No, I am not 'being ripped off' by Bob. How could he take money out of the account if there wasn't any in there, except a hundred dollars? And apparently Swiss bank accounts just have numbers, you don't have to sign, so he did not forge your father's signature. And no, I will **not** ask to see the withdrawal slip.

I don't know why you suspect him of cheating me. How can you accuse him of ripping me off when he's offered to lend me money at a rate far below the banks? Nor is he 'trying to get in my knickers', as you so crudely put it! This is purely a business association.

Take care of yourself and let me know when you get to Lebanon.

Love from Mum xx

April 15

ATTENTION: LUCY FINDLAY (PRIVATE AND CONFIDENTIAL)

Mum and Dad are getting worse. Dad got all muddled last night in bed and didn't know where he was. When I spoke to him on the phone this morning, he was nearly crying. He was very frightened. 'What if I'm getting dementia?' he wanted to know, and I said, 'But you won't know if you've got dementia, will you?' He said, 'What if I don't know who you are when you come to visit?' and I told him, 'Then you won't know you don't know me, will you?' He said I was very comforting.

But he's getting more forgetful every day. He put the newspaper in the fridge yesterday and then tried to pretend it was a joke. It's a big worry.

Love as always, Cath

April 15

DEAR FE

I didn't know Damascus is called the Fragrant City. The gardens look just beautiful. And fancy seeing the Pope in his Popemobile. I didn't know he ever went to the Middle East. Pity you didn't think to get his autograph. But then maybe the Pope doesn't give autographs – though the Queen does. If you see him again, ask him politely.

Yes, the leaves on the old pear tree are falling. Remember how loaded it was with pears last year? It's starting to get cold here now, though it's only autumn. I don't like the frost in winter, all dry and brittle. Do you remember when you were little and the dog's droppings would freeze and your father called them barker's eggs? A barker's dozen.

It was kind of Sven to invite you to stay in his hotel in the modern part of the city. And a five-star hotel! It's a shame you're not still in the old part if there's so much to see there, but then it wouldn't have the modern amenities, I suppose. They certainly built things to last in the olden days. The Omayyad Mosque looks as good as new and you say it was built in 705 AD? I hope the robe they made you put on when you went inside was clean. You never know who might have been wearing it.

Don't worry about me lifting carpets so soon after my hernia operation. I'm fine, really. And I found lovely old polished boards under the lounge-room carpet.

I've decided to get a Persian rug. It would look nice. Pity you couldn't buy one for me, as rugs are bound to be cheaper over there, but I'd need to work out the size and colours first. And how would you get it home? It's all too complicated.

I'm sad your father had so little time in this house. We had great plans for doing it up during his retirement, and he would have loved these old boards. I had a bit of a weep when I came to the spot where he had his heart attack, but I said a little prayer and then I just ripped into the carpet. One has to move on.

In fact, I think I'm now emotionally strong enough to scatter his ashes. I'll ask Amy if she wants to fly down for the ceremony. Or do you want me to wait till you come home? I'll miss him even more after he's really gone, but I mustn't be selfish. He wanted to be scattered over the sea.

We're doing Jung in basic psychology at SPUDS. Marcus Candover says that if we understand how humans think and operate it makes life simpler. He gave me an A for my essay on People in the Street and My Opinions of Them.

Your grandma hasn't been too good lately. Her back is worrying her a lot. Her spine is crumbling away so fast it must look like desiccated coconut. It was probably caused by a lack of calcium as a child, so drink your milk, Fe.

Love from Mum xx

April 18

DEAR AMY, DWAYNE AND CHILDREN

How exciting to get an email from you from just outside Disneyland! But how awful that the girls had a fight with Marla and ran away. At least they only went round the corner to the shops.

I'm well, thanks. I hope you all are too. Sorry there's not much news from my end – I told it all to you on the phone when you rang.

Love from your mother (and Grandma) xx

April 18

DEAR FE

I've posted some Eternal Life vitamin E cream to the address you gave me in Beirut, with a 'Please hold for collection' on it. Lucy said to tell you it's excellent for rashes, cuts, bruises and any skin disorders.

Thanks for your brief email. It's nice that Sven wanted you to go to Sweden with him, but I am not sending you any more money. You need to learn to manage your money better, Fe. You already owe far too much on your credit card. I don't care if you're sure Sven is your soul-mate – so far in the last month you've met three soul-mates. And if he really is, then fate will send him back to you, sort of like a Baltic boomerang.

I've decided I want a fountain in the backyard. I was really inspired by the jpegs you sent of the Al-Azem Palace. Not that I can afford anything so grand, and one like that would look out of place in a suburban backyard anyway, but I could have a smaller version.

Nowadays a fountain is called a water feature. I saw a nice one when I took Harriet for a walk. We always stop at Gone Potty and she has a drink from one of the water features there. I don't want one with balls floating about, or those bamboo balancing things, I want an old-fashioned one with water spurting out of a cherub's mouth – something tasteful.

I must stop now and do some gardening, then make a casserole to take to Grandma and Grandpa. Grandpa is lucky to be alive. He crossed the highway on his own – apparently he just stepped out and waved his stick in the air and the traffic had to slam to a halt. He said it was 'just like Moses parting the Red Sea'. He's becoming quite reckless lately, not to mention forgetful. And muddled.

Speaking of reckless, take care of yourself.

Love from Mum xx

April 19

ATTENTION: LUCY FINDLAY (PRIVATE AND CONFIDENTIAL)

No, I am not doing the sausage samba with Bob! Sometimes you are wicked. And I wasn't implying you're a bad mother just because both your kids are living overseas. You're a good mother. Look at all the breastfeeding you did – I used to think Rohan would still be on the breast when he went to school. (I've often wondered if that's why he likes full-breasted women.) I only breastfed my two for six months. And you were much better at toilet training than I was. You had Rohan on command at nine months, remember? 'Wee, Rohan,' you'd say, and he would. So never let anyone say you weren't a good mother.

Remember when I used to come and clean your house because you hated cleaning, and you'd cook exotic things for me to take home because you loved cooking? That's called skill-sharing nowadays. We invented it and we didn't even know.

Fe caught the bus from Damascus to Beirut because the rail system was unusable due to damage caused by something or other. She says French is spoken widely in the Middle East. Luckily she did French at school. Remember when Helene used to spout French and tell everyone she went to a French finishing school, and then we found out it was actually a public school in French's Forest?

I went over to Mum and Dad's last night before dinner and Mum was in a lot of pain with her back, so I switched on the oven, put the casserole in and told Dad to take it out after twenty minutes. At about nine o'clock, Mum felt the house getting hotter and hotter. She went to investigate and found the oven still on.

Dad said to her, 'Cath told me to take out the casserole, she didn't say anything about turning off the oven.' His muddle-headedness is starting to get me down. Then I feel guilty that I feel annoyed.

But on one level his brain's still ticking over. You know that ancient ute of his? It's fifty years old and the value goes up each year. He runs the engine every couple of weeks since he can't drive it, and I borrow it every now and then. Well, someone must have told Robert it was worth money, because he's been on at Dad to sell it. You know what he's like: 'It's just wasting money in rego and insurance. I'll take it off your hands for you.' Of course, Robert wouldn't be seen dead driving it, he just wants to sell it and keep the money.

Sometimes I wonder if he was adopted. He doesn't seem to have Mum or Dad's genes at all, he's so mean-spirited. He likes the high life, but if he'd married Mona McConachy and not Helene I'm sure he wouldn't have turned out such a snob.

Anyway, Dad's onto him. He told me Robert offered him two thousand for the ute, then he said, 'He doesn't know that I know it's worth twelve.' And now you won't believe this, but he's given the ute to me. So then of course I got the phone call from Robert demanding I sell it and give him half the proceeds. No way am I selling it, even if it's worth a million. I love that old ute. It has a sort of Dad smell about it, maybe it's the old leather seat, I don't know.

I did offer to pay Dad the market value (I'd have taken out a loan), but he said, 'Just repay me with casseroles.' Let's face it, I couldn't cook that many casseroles in a lifetime, but I think Dad would rather blow up the ute than let Robert get his hands on it.

It really makes Dad mad and Mum sad that Robert and Helene don't visit unless they want something. The last time they came, they had their eyes on Granny Potts's old stuff, which Mum thinks is just junk. I must warn her not to give them any of it. They'll only sell it to an antique shop, and it should stay in the family. The jewellery will get passed down to the grandchildren, so Robert and Helene can't get their greedy hands on that, thank goodness.

Must go. Oh, I got another postcard of Westminster Abbey from Jane, with 'Having a lovely time. Love, Jane. P.S. I'll be home soon.' I think she must be having a cow of a time, actually, whether she's been to Westminster Abbey or not.

Love as always, Cath

April 20

Dear Fe

Okay, I'll think about getting 'a hunk with muscles' to do the digging for the deck stumps, but I haven't got council approval yet. I can't just whack up a deck in the backyard. Bob knows someone who works in planning and says he can probably get the plans through pretty quickly, seeing it'll only be a simple deck. It's not going to destroy the ambience of the place like some ghastly extensions do. There's a chap up the street who pulled the back section off a lovely 100-year-old house and let it fall into disrepair. Now there's a notice in the front garden stating that he intends to demolish it and build a two-storey house with a lap pool. Have you ever heard of anything so ridiculous? The neighbours have taken up a petition to stop him, and I signed it willingly.

I'm fed up with selfish people doing what they want

without any regard for history and other people's feelings. This is a heritage street with lovely old miners' cottages. Modern two-storey houses can look quite nice in the right setting – but not here. Even Grandma and Grandpa have the same threat hanging over them from Uncle Robert; though luckily they don't know that.

Grandpa was telling me just the other day about some sneaky developer in the next street. He was told to keep the original structure and only build on at the back. He built a big extension, waited for a while, then deliberately damaged the front verandah post, told the council the original structure was dangerous and knocked it down. And there, ready and waiting, was a pretentious portico. Not exactly appropriate for this neighbourhood.

Enough from me on my soap-box! Back to the work around this house. You know I have a bad history with muscly hunks. The one who was meant to do the garage was unreliable. He didn't turn up when he was supposed to, then when he did he went to sleep behind the pear tree. The next one I hired tried to chat up Boris next door. He'd be leaning over the fence saying things like, 'You've got wonderful biceps.' I was so embarrassed.

In fact it's so difficult to get tradesmen nowadays that it's easier to do it myself. That's why I'm going on to do

Advanced Handywoman next, and I'll continue with SPUDS and weight-resistance classes. I need to get smarter and stronger.

Oh, you'll never guess, Aunt Helene and Uncle Robert actually dropped in unexpectedly. They'd been to a friend's place at Queenscliff for dinner, and they popped in here after visiting Grandpa and Grandma. Of course, I was up to my armpits in grot. My hair was standing straight off my head the way it does when it needs a cut. I had on a T-shirt I'd ripped on a nail, and those glue-smeared track-suit pants I should have thrown out years ago. I'd been painting the hall and there was mess everywhere. I didn't have any home-made cakes or biscuits, only stale Tim Tams, and I'd run out of fresh milk.

Aunt Helene was wearing a beige pantsuit. Not a speck of dirt on her. She had a good look around and kept saying, 'Oh, how quaint.' Uncle Robert has left Davis, Spaniel & Beggs and set up his own business. He gave me his card: 'Robert E. Miller, Financial Adviser', with his phone and email, miller@millermoney.com. He even has his own website. If you need financial advice, though, I'd go to Bob rather than your uncle. Putting Uncle Robert in charge of your finances could be a bit risky, as he hasn't much experience running his own business yet.

Did you get an email from Amy? It sounds like they're having a wonderful time in Los Angeles and surrounds. Are the curds pasteurised in rural Lebanon?

Love from Mum xx

April 22

Dear Fe

I do realise that things are more expensive in Beirut because it's a big city, but you'll just have to learn to budget. Eat the local food if it's cheaper, rather than all that American stuff – but make sure you boil everything. Not doing that is why you have the runs. Do you want me to express-mail you some pills? And don't sit on the toilet seats. They're always crawling with germs.

According to Bob, the taxation department is inquiring about your father's money affairs now. It's all too much for me, but Bob said I'm not to worry, he'll sort it out. He's doing very well since he took over the business from Henry Sims. The other night he took me out to dinner and then to a play called *Mother Love*. We went in his brand-new black BMW. It had that lovely new-car smell, and a sun roof.

I'm embarrassed to say that I fell asleep during the play because it was a bit complicated and I was worn out from being a handywoman. I found two rotten floorboards in the hallway, which I can replace, I guess, and at least the whole floor isn't rotten, but then I had nightmares about termites and woke at three a.m. I was sure I could hear them munching away in the second bedroom.

Small problems seem mountainous in the middle of the night, but now things are in perspective again and I've decided to buy a runner for the hallway and just plug up the rotten boards with something.

Your grandfather's sight is getting worse. He went for a walk the other day and a lady was bending over pulling out weeds on her nature strip. He poked her with his walking stick as he went by, and when she yelped he got a real fright. He says he thought she was a rubbish bin. That's pretty bad, even for him.

I got a fright myself when you said my emails could be read by strangers in cyberspace. I don't think I want the general public knowing about my personal details and portfolios and your grandpa porking strange women.

Love from Mum xx

April 24

Dear Fe

Are you quite sure there are no nice, cheaper hotels in Beirut? What about a Budget hotel? Or Best Western? All right, just this once I'll put extra money in your account, but make sure you get clean, decent accommodation and eat a cooked brekky and a decent evening meal, especially if you don't have much for lunch. If you're going into the desert, wear your hat and SF30 or you'll come back looking like a dried walnut.

On Monday I'm going to Lucy's womb-burying ceremony. She's had her womb in the freezer for nearly a year, waiting until Tibby can be here. You remember Lucy's daughter? She's about Amy's age and is modelling in New York. She'll be in Melbourne briefly for a job and is coming down here afterwards.

You probably think it's weird burying a womb, but it's very significant for Lucy. It's out with the old and in with the new, as she puts it, which doesn't mean she's getting a womb transplant, it means a new life. Apparently a lot of women bury their wombs after hysterectomies nowadays. We're going to bury it on the headland near Limeburner's Bay, so it will have a view over the sea. A womb with a view, as Lucy said.

Must go.

Love from Mum xx

P.S. Do you need anything?

April 26

Dear Amy

It's lovely to be able to chat on the phone now you're back home. Yes, I'll send Georgia a little something for coming equal third out of twenty in her tap class.

I do appreciate what you and Dwayne are trying to do for the girls. I know you think your social growth was stunted because you didn't do all those things when you were a child, but your father and I just didn't have the money. He was just starting his printing business at that stage and he didn't become successful until you were in your teens. And you wouldn't really have wanted to do tap and callisthenics and violin and ballet and all those things, would you? Anyway, tell the girls I am very proud of them.

Love from your mother xx

April 29

ATTENTION: LUCY FINDLAY (PRIVATE AND CONFIDENTIAL)

Who on earth would have written 'Lucy Findlay wants to FIND A LAY' on the women's toilet wall? I don't blame you for being upset. Although, well, you *do* tend to act a bit eager sometimes, you know. I appreciate that you're looking for your soul-mate (just like Fe), but I don't think one-night stands really result in a soul-mateship. I know the womb burial means a lot to you, but don't expect everything to somehow change as a result. As your best friend I can only say that's up to you, not the universe.

Speaking of the universe and heavenly things, Dad's been going on about the right to die and why God won't take him now. I thought I'd shock him out of the idea so I said, 'There's a theory that God doesn't decide it, that we actually choose when we die.' So Dad said, 'Well, I'm sick of being old and pathetic and I choose to bump myself off tonight.' Of course, Mum and I thought it was his dementia talking and didn't pay much attention. We didn't know that months ago one of his cronies had told him that the best way to achieve instantaneous death was to drink a bottle of whiskey and then walk into the freezing Southern Ocean. So last night, apparently, when Mum was asleep, Dad got a bottle of whiskey from the cupboard, walked to the main road and hailed a taxi to take him to Torquay. He sat on the sand and drank half the bottle, then decided that life wasn't so bad after all! So he came home again. Sigh. He's getting worse. I just don't know what to do.

See you next Monday. It's great that Jane's finally back and will be there too. But will we recognise her? Small miaow.

Love as always, Cath

May 3

Dear Fe

Lucy's womb-burying ceremony was so touching. There was Lucy, Peg-down-the-road, Jane, who's back from overseas, and Sandra Wisenbone, who did the ceremony (she's an official womb-burying celebrant). Lucy had her womb in a satin-lined box. Sandra read a poem for relinquished wombs, and Lucy buried it right on the cliff face. Then we had wine and nibbles sitting on the cliff-top, as a sort of wake.

Did I tell you Jane has had plastic surgery? An extreme makeover. They lifted her face and the baggy skin under her chin, and the bump on the end of her nose has been smoothed out. She also had liposuction and a tummy tuck. I couldn't tell if she's had the fat on her upper arms done, as she was wearing long sleeves.

She said the procedure's called 'resculpting', and as she'd inherited money from an aunt, and some of the world's best surgeons are in London doing nips and tucks on movie stars, she thought, Why not? Why not indeed. Except that now she makes Lucy and I look like the Haggard Sisters.

Speaking of haggard, Tibby looked rather haggard as well, but I suppose most models are a bit gaunt. She also looked stressed, but then Lucy's womb was her home for nine months, so I guess there could have been some unresolved inner-child issues, as Lucy said.

I don't know about this Habid person, dear. Taking you to a remote part of the desert sounds dangerous, especially if there weren't many women there. But I'm pleased to hear that the Lebanese are very courteous, even if not many of them seem to speak English. I've never heard of the Jeita Grotto, even though you say it's one of the most amazing caves in the world. Travel certainly broadens the mind. And you're now going to Tripoli by bus and coming back on a ferry? Do be careful, I've heard they pack people in like sardines, so don't get on an overcrowded boat, will you?

Your grandfather got it into his head to go for a ride on his old bike the other day. Of course the tyres were flat, and he ran into the gutter, fell off and got a grazed lip and an egg on his head. It was lucky he'd left his top teeth in a glass at home or he would have put them right through his lower lip.

Your grandma is shrinking before my eyes, and there's nothing the doctors can do. I heard on talkback that almonds are full of calcium, so eat lots of almonds as well as drinking milk.

As for me, my arches seem to have dropped. I went to the podiatrist and he said I need orthotics. I hope my bones aren't crumbling, although my bone-density test went well. I've had my hormone prescription readjusted, so I shouldn't get as many hot flushes. I hope I don't put on more weight.

As well as weight-resistance classes I've joined Prime Movers. It's exercises and aerobics for people over fifty. We do a lot of pelvic-floor exercises. You should do them too. It's quite easy, really – you just clench yourself until you could hold a tram ticket between your buttocks, hold for a count of ten, then release. You're supposed to do fifty a day. Today I did them in the bank queue. The woman behind me was complaining about the wait and I whispered, 'Do some pelvic-floor exercises.' Quite a few people seemed to take up the idea, judging from their expressions. I felt a bit like Crusader Rabbit, changing the world in the bank queue.

Love from Mum xx

May 4

DEAR AMY

Are you remembering to do your pelvic-floor exercises? You could have inherited my weak bladder. Most women do them while they're pregnant but then give up – I can send you a pamphlet if you can't remember. And how are your arches?

It's wonderful that Sydney is now an official Turtle. Thank you for the jpegs of the children, especially the boys – they look very cute.

Love from your mother x

May 4

ATTENTION: LUCY FINDLAY (PRIVATE AND CONFIDENTIAL)

Your ceremony was wonderful. I hope it helped. But Jane's 'resculpting' – a bit much, don't you think? The skin on her cheekbones looks too tight. And did you notice that one of her eyebrows is higher than the other? Don't tell her, or she'll be on the next plane back to London. But she is lovely and slim, with a stomach to die for. I asked her if she was worried the fat would come back, and she said it never comes back to the same place. She could get fat ears, I suppose.

I still think something's wrong between her and Derek. She seemed miserable, despite looking twenty years younger than us. If I had a bottom and thighs like hers, I'd be radiant. I phoned today to see if she'd like a coffee and chat, but Derek said she was asleep, and that was at noon. Maybe she's still jetlagged, but I'm quite worried about her. She's just not the same Jane. She was preoccupied before she left for the UK, but she seems to have gone right into her shell now she's back. Do you think she's embarrassed about her new looks? You'd think she'd be flaunting them, and raving about London, but she hardly said a word yesterday. And I still think it was odd her not telling us about it beforehand.

Anyway, I asked Derek to tell her to call me but she hasn't. I'll phone again tonight.

I thought you looked lovely and slim yourself in those new black pants. Brisbane sounds even busier than Melbourne, all those sales meetings you have to attend. They'd drive me bonkers. And so much dashing about – too hectic for me.

Love as always, Cath

May 7

Dear Fe

So now you're in Israel? I thought you were going to Jordan. I'm a bit confused. But Jo sounds nice and sensible, so it's good you're going to Egypt with her. I'm glad you've bought some Middle Eastern robes. Who cares if you look like Casper the Friendly Ghost? It's not good to wear tight jeans in hot countries – you're likely to get a yeast infection.

Your Uncle Robert and Aunt Helene have bought a new black Mercedes with leather seats. You know how Aunt Helene often has a forced smile? When Grandpa heard about the new car he said, 'Well, her smile might be plastic but at least her backside's sitting on leather now.' He can be quite naughty at times. And wonder of wonders, Aunt Helene came to visit your grandparents again. I think she probably just wanted to show off the car, because she called in here again too and asked if I'd like to go shopping with her. In the Mercedes. I didn't really want to, seeing as I'd been shopping with Pam the day before, but I said yes.

She also wanted to borrow the silver tea service that belonged to Great-Granny Potts – for some charity heirloom afternoon, she said – but I told her it really belongs to you. So if she emails you (she asked for your address) don't answer. I doubt they'd ever give it back and it's worth a fair bit, you know, being so old. I can't imagine her displaying it on her ultra-modern shelving, can you?

Anyway, we went into a boutique and I saw this lovely warm coat in a beige shade, but Aunt Helene said I looked a bit like a toadstool in it and that you'd have to be tall, slim and blonde to wear it. So *she* bought it! I guess it does help when you're tall, slim and blonde. I don't know how she does it. I only have to look at food and I put on weight. Even the dog is getting fatter. But then Aunt Helene only had black coffee for afternoon tea, while I had two scones with jam and cream, so that could explain it.

Amazing. I've got the council approval for my deck already, and have started buying the materials. But I'm getting a termite inspector in first. I couldn't sleep last night for the munching.

Love from Mum xx

May 10

Dear Fe

I had a feeling Uncle Robert would email to ask for the silver tea service, but what a cheek to suggest he manage your finances as well! It was clever of you to delete the email without answering, as then he might just think you never got it.

I wish you could be a fly on the wall at our Prime Movers classes. We do Pump, which is full-on – step aerobics, marching on the spot holding light weights, tummy work and leg work, all to fast music. We're certainly all puffing at the end.

The Prime Movers come in all shapes and sizes. Pam has a muscular sort of shape. She desperately wanted to be a ballerina when she was a kid, but she was too short and stocky. Then there's a large lady called Marion who does nothing but moan. If our instructor says we're going to try lunges, Marion immediately says, 'What about my tricky knee?' If it's time to do calf-raises, she'll say, 'I can't do this because of my tricky ankle.' We come to the thigh exercises and of course Marion says, 'I have a tricky thigh.' Every single part of her body has something wrong with it.

We've also got an 83-year-old who's so skinny she looks like a grasshopper in her green tracksuit. She leaps and bounces about like she's on an adrenaline drip. There's a man whose feet smell, another one who makes grunting noises every time he moves, and me staggering about like a uncoordinated zombie – it could be a TV comedy, really.

Our instructor Rona is very particular about everything we do. Of course this is important, because by the time people are in their fifties they usually have a history of past injuries and we could damage ourselves even more. We have to provide a medical certificate before we start the classes. Yesterday we were working with large Swisse balls. We had to sit on them, then walk our feet out until only our heads and shoulders were on the ball. It was very hard to balance. Rona was correcting me. 'Lift your hips. Pull in your stomach. Walk your feet out further.' Then in exasperation, 'Cath, *where is your bottom?*' I said, 'Hanging down,' which made everyone laugh. Well, it was!

Today was a nearly perfect day for being outside. I took Harriet for a long walk to the Botanical Gardens, then I managed to get all the lawns mowed, plus old Fred-across-the-way's nature strip, and then two hours later it poured. I took two roast dinners up to Grandpa and Grandma. Grandpa said, 'At last, roast lamb. I thought we'd sold it all to the Arabs.' You'd think he hadn't eaten roast lamb for years, but he had it only a week ago.

I really need to do something about your father's ashes. The other day I left the urn on the sofa after I'd been watching TV and Bob accidentally sat on it. He was so embarrassed, and very kind and comforting when I started to cry.

'Cath,' he said, 'I know what it's like when someone you love has gone and isn't coming back.' I think I told you that his wife ran off with her personal trainer and now they're divorced.

So I really think I'll have to scatter the ashes without you, dear. I'll ask Amy to fly down. I hope you don't mind.

Love from Mum xx

May 12

Dear Amy

Thank you for your email, although I'm very sorry you can't come to your father's disposal ceremony. I understand you're worried about the terrorist threat, but you didn't seem too worried about flying to Disneyland. And what about your sister in the Middle East? Surely that's more threatening? Anyway, if you don't want to come to your father's ash-scattering, it's okay. I'll pay your respects to him myself.

Love from your mother x

May 14

LUCY FINDLAY (PRIVATE AND CONFIDENTIAL)

You don't need to be upset because you suddenly have to go to Perth and can't come to the ashes-scattering.

Pam can't come either, because she's having a breast-cancer examination. Just routine, nothing sinister. But I dread getting squashed under that glass plate thing, don't you? They can fly rockets to Mars but they can't invent a painless breast examination. I bet if men's penises had to be squashed like that, someone would find a painless method in a flash.

Bob's away on business again, otherwise he would have come for your father's sake. One of Gaye's boys is graduating that day, so she can't make it either, nor can Sandra or Peg. But Jane said she'll come.

I phoned her and we met for coffee. She finally confessed that things aren't too good with Derek. It's nothing she can put her finger on, she claims, they're not fighting or anything like that, but she said Derek's been withdrawn and their sex life is practically non-existent. She thinks there might be another woman, which is why she had her makeover. New body, new face, new see-through lingerie, but still no sex!

It certainly sounds like there could be someone else,

but I didn't want to upset her so I just said this kind of thing often happens when men get older; that men get anxious because they can't perform and then they avoid it. She said, 'How do you know that?' and I said, 'Talkback radio, and also James was like that for a while until he got his prostate fixed.'

Anyway, the good news is that she's coming with me to scatter the ashes, which is really kind of her. Must dash. Have fun and be good.

Love as always, Cath xx

May 14

DEAR FE

Thank you for being so understanding about me going ahead with your father's ashes. I'm sure he'd forgive you for not being there. I held off so Amy could come, now that they're back from America, but she's worried about terrorists on the plane. I suggested the train, but she had an excuse for that too. I don't think she can cope with the idea of seeing your father's remains in ash form.

I've organised to go out on the ferry tomorrow with Jane and we'll scatter the ashes over the side.

I noticed in the last photos you sent that you're still

wearing jeans. If you do get a yeast infection, use yoghurt (plain, not fruit).

I actually bought some new jeans for myself. Do you think fifty-five is too old for stretch jeans? I hope not. I don't want to look like mutton dressed as lamb. I must admit I've always hated new jeans, they take forever to break in and get comfy. So I bought second-hand ones from the op shop. Pregnancy jeans are best, because there's a big turnover. People get rid of them after they've had the baby, so they're almost brand-new. And no one can tell they're maternity jeans if I wear a shirt over the top.

Love from Mum xx

May 19

ATTENTION: LUCY FINDLAY (PRIVATE AND CONFIDENTIAL)

Thanks for the ashes-scattering card and roses. I got a real surprise when the florist arrived at the door. It was lovely of you to think of me when you're so busy in Perth.

Love as always, Cath

May 19

DEAR AMY

Yes, I do understand that you were too upset to come to the ceremony. It all went really well, and now your father is truly at peace on the high seas. It was upsetting, but I feel that I now have closure.

Love from your mother x

May 19

DEAR FE

Well, it's done. Jane and I took your father on the ten a.m. ferry from Queenscliff to Sorrento. Luckily it wasn't too busy that time of morning. We both wore black. I had on my good suit – the one with the longer jacket that you helped me choose, remember? – and Jane wore an astrakhan coat she bought in London.

It all went swimmingly. When the ferry was about halfway across the bay we walked to the front, a bit like in *Titanic*, and I said, 'Ashes to ashes, dust to dust,' then I lifted the lid and scattered the ashes. The only bad thing was that the wind was blowing into our faces. Well, it was actually a westerly blowing from behind – we'd checked that – but evidently there's something on boats called apparent winds. Most of the ashes blew back over us, and on a bunch of Japanese tourists who were standing nearby. Jane said, 'Holy hell,' which wasn't exactly appropriate, but then fortunately the apparent wind turned and blew your father into the sea, so all was well.

Fe, are you truly happy living this hand-to-mouth existence? Won't you consider coming home earlier than planned, seeing as money is becoming a problem? You're still not telling me how you feel. Maybe you're too embarrassed to discuss your feelings? I'm not embarrassed about my own: I miss your father and feel very sad, even though there's closure, but things are more of a fuzzy grey than black now. Hope you're feeling more grey than black too.

Love from Mum xx

May 23

Dear Fe

I'm sorry I shocked you writing about your father's ashes, but as I said they did eventually blow into the sea. Sometimes I feel as if his ghost is visiting me to see how I'm going. I don't see him, of course, it's just a feeling that he's here.

Jane says it's the energy field that he left, and there are no such things as ghosts. Lucy says we should hold a seance, but Pam says to leave well enough alone. I haven't mentioned any of this to Sandra Wisenbone, who's so uptight about anything supernatural she couldn't even sit through *Ghostbusters*. Though she did conduct Lucy's womb-burying with great aplomb. She seems to enjoy that side of death.

Bob hasn't found my missing money, although he's still on its trail. He suggested a while back that I need to get a bit wiser when it comes to money, even though he's been helping me make decisions, so Pam, Gaye and I booked into three short courses: Roll Over in the Clover, Wealth and You, and Manage Your Money. But all they seemed to care about was selling us life-insurance policies and superannuation. It's a bit late for that now. I also went to Shares for Success, but shares are complicated.

According to Peg-down-the-road, there are some pluses about getting older. I'll get a Senior's Card and will be able to get discounts on public transport and at the movies. She went to Sydney on the overnight train from Melbourne and got around Sydney on ferries and trains and buses for the day for a special rate – two dollars, I think she said.

You really must stop worrying about Bob ripping me

off, Fe. He's an extremely honest man. I hope you're not squandering your own money.

Yesterday in psychology we had a go at some creative writing. It's supposed to help get your feelings out and link your creativity to your subconscious. Marcus was quite impressed with my little story for kids about an elf who dances through the forest picking up cans. Marcus thinks I have a repressed need to pick up other people's garbage. And I've started keeping a sort of journal, with short poems and little jottings about everyday things.

Love from Mum xx

May 24

Dear Fe

I must say I was getting a bit sick of your comments about Bob, so I plucked up the courage to ask him how much he paid for the BMW, as you suggested. He said it's leased and it's paid for by the business. So much for your suspicious mind!

I trust him completely. And if he was stealing my money, why would he encourage me to go to seminars to learn how to manage it? But even though I went to those seminars, I still don't know enough about investing and

I have to trust someone, don't I? You know, you'd really like Bob if you met him. He looks a bit like your father, only shorter and plumper and balder.

I'm a bit confused as to where you're going next. Riding around the Sea of Galilee, then going to Tiberius and meeting up with the backpackers you travelled with in Turkey sounds nice. But I've looked up Petra on the map and it seems a complicated way to get to Egypt.

Did I tell you I'm flying up to Sydney again, this time for Dakota's birthday party? I've bought him some board shorts and a planks-and-ladders puzzle and three lovely books. And I'll give Amy some money to put in his bank account. Don't forget to send him a present. You know how upset your sister gets when you forget the childrens' birthdays.

Yes, I know I listen to a lot of talkback radio. I have difficulty sleeping at night. I go to bed around ten-thirty and fall asleep immediately, but then I wake up again about two and can't get back to sleep. Apparently this is another common menopausal complaint. There are a lot of sleepless people out there, you know, and the things they discuss are amazing – warts, house prices, waffle cones, mosquito larvae, and all sorts of personal problems.

The other day, Peg-down-the-road invited me to a

seniors' lunch. I was the youngest person there. Everyone seemed to be over seventy, and starving. They ate like there was no tomorrow. Sandwiches, barbecued chicken, quiches, meatballs – all disappearing faster than a magician's rabbit. And they all had their handbags over their arms so they could take the leftovers home in paper napkins.

Your grandma could have gone, but she thinks that crowd's a bit old for her. I know you're thinking, Well, she's eighty-six – but she feels she's young at heart and those people all think old. That's what she says. I'd take her to bingo on Thursday afternoons, but she always yells 'Bingo' before she's filled in the squares. It's a bit embarrassing.

Love from Mum xx

May 27

ATTENTION: LUCY FINDLAY (PRIVATE AND CONFIDENTIAL)

Dear God, I wish Fe would get out of the Middle East before I get an ulcer from the worry. They've been fighting there for centuries, and they're not going to suddenly stop because Fiona Morgan's there, are they?

On another note, I've come to agree with you that I

probably need a social life, so – are you sitting down? – Gaye and I are going out to dinner with two men on Friday night! I still love James, even though he's dead, and I don't want to have a casual fling – the thought of it me makes me feel quite uncomfortable – but these two are decent, unmarried men. Gaye knows because she got them through an agency. And we're all going together, so it'll be safe.

I'll let you know how it goes.

Love as always, Cath

May 27

Dear Amy

Yes, I've booked my flight on fly-buys, thanks to all the wood and nails and paint I've been buying recently. See you soon.

Love from your mother x

May 29

Dear Fe

Well, you've certainly been all over the place in a very short time. Haifa and Tel Aviv, then the Dead Sea. I was intrigued to hear about Jerusalem and the Wailing Wall, and that they haven't got a plaque saying where Jesus lived. Someone phoned up talkback the other night and said Melbourne should have a Wailing Wall at Southbank so people can cry over taxes and the demolition of historic buildings. I'm so glad you're out of Israel now, because I heard on the news that a woman tied a bomb to herself and blew up a busload of people.

Speaking of bombs, I had a bombshell dropped on me by Uncle Robert. He's demanding that I split the silver tea service and china and give him half because they're part of the family estate. Did you ever hear anything so silly? He says he's had legal advice! I don't dare tell Grandma and Grandpa, they'd be so upset – Grandpa would probably have a heart seizure. I've discussed this with Bob, who thinks Uncle Robert's bluffing. Bob says he'll talk to a solicitor friend; he doesn't think your uncle has any right to these things, because they were gifts.

But it all leaves a sour taste in my mouth. Fighting over possessions makes me feel quite ill. I suspect Uncle Robert is peeved because I won't give him all my millions (ha ha) to manage. I suggest you continue to ignore any emails from him and Aunt Helene. I'm sorry to involve you in all this, but if I don't tell you (ditto with Amy), you could get sucked into some scheme or other.

I think I told you that I've got permission from the council to build the deck? Bob's coming round on Saturday to help me dig the stump holes. Let me know if you need anything, won't you, and don't go diving into the Nile when you get to Egypt. I've heard the water's not at all clean.

Love from Mum xx

May 29

Dear Amy

Uncle Robert sent me the same brochures, followed by a phone call. He can't really think we're going to hand all our money over to him in the hope he'll make a big profit for us. As you know, he does not have a good track record with other people's money, so I strongly advise you not to give him any.

Thanks for sending the drawing of a red truck with purple tyres that Dakota did in Penguins. I'll put it on the fridge.

Love from your mother x

May 30

Attention: Lucy Findlay (Private and Confidential)

Robert really has got a nerve. He wants half of Granny Potts's things that Mum and Dad have given me, and of course half the ute. I wouldn't trust him with my piggy bank, let alone a portfolio of shares and my term deposits. Luckily Bob is sorting it out for me.

Meanwhile, I could wring Fe's neck! I've done what you suggested and have remained calm and interested when I email her, but she's just been on a so-called organised tour in the desert and the truck ran out of petrol. How organised is that? She just floats about in that dangerous part of the world, totally oblivious. I'll end up with ulcers and a heart attack and then she'll wish she'd listened to me.

And so much for a new social life. Our dinner date was a disaster. Gaye's man was as dreary as dishwater – he went on and on about his divorce and how his wife ripped him off. He was bald and miserable, even though his resumé said he was handsome and GSOH, which we thought stood for 'good solid own home' but which apparently means 'good sense of humour'. He didn't have that either. What's more, he also ordered the most expensive stuff on the menu, drank martinis and double whiskies, and then expected Gaye to pay half the bill.

My date was called Evan and he was skinny and sickly. He only ate soup and a salad because of his bowel complaint. And he's on gluten-free, fat-free, dairy-free, sugar-free food and he talked all night about his operations. So Gaye and I politely told them we thought we were slightly incompatible and made our escape, although they seemed to like us a lot.

I don't think we'll be meeting any more men through that agency, but when we looked at the ads people put in the paper they were even worse. One read: 'Romantic, virile 60yo with loyal, caring and adventuresome qualities, self-employed, NS, SD, GSOH, DTE. Likes movies, wining and dining, weekends away, massages, cycling, bushwalks and beach. Looking for soul-mate who is attractive, buxom, slim, romantic, sensual, feminine, employed and wants to be romanced, cherished and loved to death.'

Gaye reckons he must be married if he only wants weekends away. I phoned the newspaper to find out what NS, SD and DTE mean, and they're non-smoker, social drinker and down-to-earth.

Another one read: 'Single man, 70yo, own home, seeks lady to live in for friendship, travel and companionship.' Gaye said he wants sex and housekeeping for free.

And what about this one: 'Done the housework,

feeling lonely and bored? I'm a 25yo male, eager to please and I have the equipment to do it, bedroom/balloon/inflatable fun. Older ladies most welcome.' Gaye said he's probably a male prostitute, although neither of us is sure about the balloons and inflatables. Maybe it's some sort of code? I mean, I'm not dumb and I know about desperate men and blow-up dolls, but what is anyone doing with a balloon?

I know some of the people who place these ads are genuinely lonely and looking for someone nice, but a lot of them sound very dubious. I told Gaye I'd rather forget finding male companionship for a while. And anyway, I've just scattered James. It doesn't seem right. She said she wants a man to flaunt in front of her ex, any man would do. Her ex and the woman he met at the Well of Silence have started a takeaway curry shop here in the main street. It's called Hot Stuff. You think he'd have the decency to go to another town, wouldn't you?

Am lunching with Jane on Tuesday, so I'll let you know if there are any new developments.

Love as always, Cath

May 31

DEAR FE

It will be lovely when you get to Egypt proper. I've always wanted to see the pyramids and the Nile myself, but instead I'm going to Dakota's birthday party this weekend. Did I tell you that after we scattered your father's ashes, three dolphins appeared and swam with the ferry? When I told Lucy she said it was a good omen, that dolphins are actually human spirits in disguise. Or maybe it was ancient sea gods? Anyway, it was a good omen.

Life is busy here. The stumps for the deck are in and the timber has arrived, so I can start putting on the planks. Gaye and Pam have been helping, and Bob has been great with his new nail gun. He's just bought the freehold of a new commercial building and is setting up in part of it himself and leasing out the other offices. He's been putting in some new shelving, hence the new nail gun.

Gaye and Pam and I have become firm friends. Gaye is having a hard time with her husband being back in town. Pam's a widow like me, but unlike Dad, her husband had a slow and terrible death from bone cancer. So sad.

I don't know what's worse, to have someone taken from you without warning, like your father was, or slowly and agonisingly, like Pam's husband. She said in a way it was good because they could talk about the future and get things organised, and they discussed what he wanted at his funeral. He wanted 'Rhinestone Cowboy' instead of the 23rd Psalm!

Funerals cost an arm and a leg nowadays. I thought of getting a prepaid one for myself, but as Bob says, why give the money to the funeral parlour to invest when he could be investing it for me?

My shares are apparently not doing too well at the moment, but at least I won't have to pay much tax. Anyway, Bob has everything under control. He tells me the share market will recover, but I still think it'd be a good idea to get a part-time job so that I'll have more cashflow. But I haven't worked for thirty years and I'm not sure what I could do. I might ask Lucy.

Poor Lucy is still having bad luck with men. Grandpa had a bit of a turn because he took two water pills instead of his heart pill, but he's okay now.

Love from Mum xx

May 31

ATTENTION: LUCY FINDLAY (PRIVATE AND CONFIDENTIAL)

I haven't told you before, but I've been corresponding by email with an interesting man. His name is Esra Mann, he's in his fifties, and he has a pilot's licence and his own plane. He sent me a photo of himself – grey-haired and quite distinguished-looking.

Esra is a bit of an adventurer, and a widower. Twice. His first wife died on a trek in the Himalayas and his second wife died in a plane crash in the Amazon jungle. He managed to walk away unscathed, but his heart has been broken. He connected to me when I mistyped the email address of a hardware supplier and it somehow went to him by mistake. At the moment he's in Peru visiting ancient Inca temples. Isn't that exciting?

Sounds like you're leading a pretty adventurous life these days, too. Like meeting Percy the millionaire when your skirt got caught in the revolving door at the conference in Perth. And being taken to a posh restaurant and quaffing Dom Perigon, Russian caviar, lobster and Swiss chocolates. It's like something out of Mills & Boon. What a dream guy he sounds – polite, generous, and lovely aftershave. And a mansion on the Swan River.

But I can't believe you saw him using a penis pump in the ensuite! I don't blame you for feeling let down. Still, even though he turned out to be a real flop on one level, so to speak, couldn't you just forget the sex and learn to love him without the physical contact? Or get used to the pump? I know you enjoy sex, but it isn't everything.

Sigh. Okay, so I guess Percy isn't the one for you, but Mr Right is out there somewhere. Come out, come out, wherever you are! Fe says she isn't looking for Mr Right, but I'm sure deep down all women are, if they haven't already found him. I know where my Mr Right is, floating in Bass Strait by now. Sorry, I'm getting a bit maudlin again.

Since I'm in need of some cash at the moment, Pam, Gaye and I are going to take a stall at the Sunday market. We're sharing the cost of the stall hire, and Pam's made little deck chairs for kids out of material with cute motifs of Thomas the Tank Engine and Pooh Bear and others. Gaye's made some arty-looking plant containers out of various widths and lengths of aluminium pipe. I'm selling some of those plates I did years ago in my china-painting phase, and some of my indoor pot plants, since I have too many as it is and less and less time to look after them.

I just had an email from Fe. She's going to Luxor and the pyramids and then she wants to go up the Nile. Now she's in Egypt I've calmed down a bit. I think it's more stable there, not so much political and religious strife.

Hope you're okay, Stay nice! I'm off to Sydney for

Dakota's birthday. Who knows, I might meet a rich, intelligent man on the plane. But then pigs might fly.

Love as always, Cath

June 3

DEAR FE

I had a wonderful time in Sydney. Dwayne met me at the airport on Saturday morning and I didn't have to blow up balloons or prepare party food because they'd hired Kidz Parties again. This time it was a nursery-rhyme theme. Dakota had on a little Humpty Dumpty costume they'd hired. He was so funny – when all his guests started to arrive, he rushed out yelling 'Happy birthday!'

A couple of the mothers got a bit snooty with each other because their boys were both dressed as Little Jack Horner. Apparently Calum's mother had told Harris's mother that Calum was going as Old King Cole. All up, there were twenty little boys running screaming through the house and riding their plastic trikes and cars down the driveway. Then Arclay (he was dressed as Wee Willie Winkie) crashed into the letterbox and Amy decided they were getting too silly. Mind you, no one knew she was upset because she maintained a calm exterior, but I knew because her nostrils got that pinched look. After the bike-riding, Dwayne was kept busy trying to stop the boys from drowning in the fishpond.

They had a magician too, but I suspect he was drunk because his breath stank of beer and he kept dropping his magic cards. Still, the kids thought he was funny. They had games, and then Horatio pushed Dakota off the retaining wall, seeing as he was supposed to be Humpty Dumpty. Luckily Dakota wasn't hurt.

I was exhausted by the end of it. I took lots of photos, so I'll send you some. I must buy one of those digital cameras. Your photos of Mt Sinai were very interesting. Who is the tall, dark man with his arm round you? I mean the really dark one. I hope your yeast infection is better.

Love from Mum x

June 5

ATTENTION: LUCY FINDLAY (PRIVATE AND CONFIDENTIAL)

I can't believe how quickly the year is going. I had a lovely time in Sydney, but I can only stand it for a few days. The children are all so active. And I had to get a qualified carer for Mum and Dad as well as having Peg-down-the-road drive over to check on them.

The girls are becoming more and more of a handful for Amy. They demand designer clothes and the latest toys, and keep threatening to phone their mother if they don't get what they want. I said to Amy, 'Let them phone their mother, she might take them off your hands.' Amy said, 'I don't want them taken off my hands. It would absolutely shatter Dwayne to lose his girls, and I'm pleased that they take an interest in their appearance. I don't want them dressed in cheap stuff anyway.' I said, 'Cheap stuff was good enough for you.'

You know I love Virginia and Georgia, but really, they're turning into bossy little tyrants. Dwayne isn't there a lot, he's usually travelling for work, so the brunt of it falls on Amy. I'm proud of the way she's taken on a ready-made family as well as having her own two boys, but all that scheduling and having to keep up appearances drives me mad. I wouldn't live there if you paid me.

Did you know that Jane's back in hospital? She says she has to have surgery for her blocked nasal tubes, but I think she's having trouble with her new nose job. She's only in for two nights. I'll send her some flowers from both of us, and maybe you could send her an Eternal Life hospital pack. That'd cheer her up. I offered to go and visit, but she said not to bother and that Derek will bring her home.

I hope it turns out okay and she doesn't end up looking like Michael Jackson.

Love as always, Cath

June 6

DEAR FE

It's sad but Grandpa is getting more and more confused. He went sleepwalking in his pyjamas the other night and got lost. Someone found him two streets away, crying in their garden, and they called the police, who brought him home. We think it's his new sleeping pills. I suggested he take some of Lucy's Eternal Life Tranquil Night capsules and he said, 'Eternal life? Don't like the sound of that! Who wants eternal life at my age? I'm looking forward to going up there and seeing all my friends again.' Grandma said to him, 'Your friends won't be up there, they'll be down there.'

Lucy has a new boyfriend. He's an actor, Conrad Winkle. Do you remember that TV mini-series *Last Hope*? Well, he was the hot-dog man who sold the serial killer the hot dog. He only had one line: 'Ketchup or mustard with that?' I hope he turns out to be good for her.

I haven't finished the deck yet, but with Gaye and Pam

and Bob helping me it won't be long. Gaye thinks Bob's really nice; in fact she flirts with him a bit, but he just winks at me and goes on with whatever he's doing. I think I told you Gaye's good at plumbing? When we did water features in handywoman class she showed a great aptitude, so she's going to help me do one here as well. Next class we're doing concrete repairs, and the week after that it's basic bricklaying.

I applied for a job in a florist's because I'm good with flowers and plants, but I didn't get it. Oh well.

Love from Mum xx

June 7

ATTENTION: LUCY FINDLAY (PRIVATE AND CONFIDENTIAL)

Yes, Jane's out of hospital. I took around a casserole and some soup and offered to do some laundry, but Derek said they were managing fine. It's hard to tell what she's had done because her nose is still bandaged, but from what I could see she had two black eyes and looked like she'd gone ten rounds with Muhammad Ali.

She loved the flowers and your hospital pack, although she can't use the face creams just at the moment. I've found I can't use any makeup or skin products myself just now, because they bring me out in a rash. I thought it was shingles at first, seeing as it's going around, but usually you get a rash on your lower abdomen, don't you? I phoned Dr Valushi and she said itchy skin and allergies can be another symptom of menopause. She asked if I had a dry vagina. I said I didn't know. She's posted me a new prescription and increased my oestrogen to 12. I've only been on it for five days and already my breasts feel like bags of concrete.

Love as always, Cath

P.S. Esra is now trekking along the Great Wall of China.

June 10

Dear Fe

Thanks for calling the other night. I'm really pleased you're enjoying Egypt. The train trip to Luxor along the Nile sounded very picturesque. Do send me a photo of Nefertiti's tomb if you come across it.

Life is still busy here. It's Great-Uncle Gordon's hundredth birthday next week, so I'm having a family party. I know half the relatives don't talk to each other, and some of them won't come if the others come, but still, it's the right thing to do. I'll apologise for you but it would be nice if you could send him a postcard, maybe with a sphinx on it, to prove you really are in Egypt. Not that he'd be able to see it that well, but I can put it on the mantelpiece.

Surprisingly, Uncle Robert and Aunt Helene accepted their invitation, but in a way I hope they don't turn up. They always seem to dampen everyone's spirits by looking down their noses. But then I must let bygones be bygones. There's been no more talk about them wanting things since Bob's solicitor friend sent them a letter telling them not to harass me about family gifts.

I had a lot of trouble buying a hundredth-birthday card. There's apparently not a big demand for them, which is understandable, I suppose, so the choice was pretty limited. Someone told me that local members of parliament are supposed to organise telegrams from the Queen and the prime minister, so I did that, and I've ordered a sponge cake. I didn't want a fruit cake in case he chokes on the nuts. It would be a dreadful twist of fate if he survived all those years and then choked to death at his hundredth-birthday party. I thought that rather than cluttering the cake with a hundred candles, I'd put a number 1 and two zeros, and he should manage to blow them out. Maybe I should borrow Peg-down-the-road's father's oxygen tank, just in case. That's one advantage of living in a suburb with older folk, they have things like oxygen tanks to hand.

Amy says she'll fly down with the children, even though she's still terrified about terrorists, because it's not every day someone turns a hundred and she wants the kids to see what someone that old looks like. Grandpa doesn't want to come because he says Great-Uncle Gordon is fibbing about his age. Apart from family, Bob will be coming, and of course Lucy, who's bringing Lombardi, and Jane and Derek and Bryan are coming too.

I must go, I have to cook dinner for Grandma and Grandpa.

Love from Mum xx

June 12

ATTENTION: LUCY FINDLAY (PRIVATE AND CONFIDENTIAL)

Oh, what fantastic news! Can't chat just now, I'm going to the market. But big fat congratulations on your engagement. It's all very sudden, isn't it, but if Lombardi is your Mr Right then it is right. Can't wait to see the ring.

Love as always, Cath

June 14

Dear Fe

Your sister had a little scare this week. They went to Woy Woy a month or so ago and then she was late. Dwayne's had his tubes tied, but apparently there's quite a failure rate with vasectomies. One man I heard on talkback had to be snipped three times. Anyway, it turns out she isn't pregnant after all. Of course it wouldn't have been the end of the earth if she was, but they wouldn't want a child called Woy Woy.

Did you know Amy has a new job at a crisis centre? It's right near Seascape Day Care. I think she counsels people contemplating suicide – I'm not sure. The hours are good, nine to five, and it's easy for her to pick up Dakota and Sydney.

Speaking of crises, Bryan got picked up for shoplifting. Jane was absolutely mortified to think that her perfect son might have committed a crime. He claimed he hadn't stolen anything, and that the two watches, the Playboy underpants and the CD accidentally fell into his pockets.

The big news is that the deck is now finished. It isn't big, only three metres by three metres, but it was a lot of work. I felt a great sense of achievement when I was finally able to sit on it. I bought some oil to bring out the grain in the timber. The weather's a bit too cold to sit on it much at the moment, but I'm busy doing the cherub water feature. I have to dig a small trench to lay the cable for the pump, so Gaye and Bob are coming round to help again.

I think Gaye's still keen on Bob, although when I asked her she said, 'He's the serious type, and I'm looking for someone for social outings, really.' But I think she'd grab him in a flash if he asked her, though he doesn't seem interested.

I went for a part-time job at the cake shop in the mall, but I didn't get it. The woman who interviewed me asked whether I'd had any experience with cakes, and being nervous I blurted out, 'Yes, eating them.' So can you please use your money sparingly. I'm not broke, but I do need to watch my spending until the shares go up. I can hear you say, But you've just bought a water feature! Well, I got it cheaply because one of the cherub's wings is a bit chipped, but it won't matter because we can turn that part to the fence.

I drove Grandpa and Grandma to Torquay on Saturday and on the way home I stopped to buy them an ice-cream. 'This is a bit of role reversal,' I said to them. 'Remember when we were little you used to drive us to Torquay and buy us ice-cream?' And Grandpa said, 'If I'd known your brother was going to turn out to be such a mean bastard, I wouldn't have bothered.'

I do love my times with Grandma and Grandpa, even though I get tired out. Who knows how long I'll have them here? You never know what's around the corner.

Speaking of sudden, Lucy's got engaged to a man called Lombardi Belladonna! She's only known him for about a minute, so it's very sudden. She says the ring is huge, a diamond. I guess I'll see it at Uncle Gordon's party, although Lombardi can't make it after all. He's in Property Development, but he's not pulling down old houses and building those awful concrete coffins. Apparently he does up old warehouses. Lucy's having a small engagement party at the Sheraton, with just a few close friends. Jane says I should buy something new to wear, but I think I'll just stick to my black dress and wear the pearls your father gave me.

Did you get the parcel I sent by express post?

Love from Mum xx

June 17

DEAR FE

Yes, I know I told you Lucy was going out with Conrad Winkle, but he turned out to be a pain in the neck. She said he was too theatrical. Everything was a drama. He just didn't seem to understand what she calls 'basic concepts of ordinary'. She met Lombardi at a single bar – apparently it was love at first sight. I do hope it works out for her this time.

Well, Great-Uncle Gordon's birthday was a huge success and everyone enjoyed themselves. Even me. Bob came along to help, which was really nice of him, although Amy wasn't too pleased about him being in the kitchen. He did look cute with the tea towel slung over his shoulder, though, a bit like your father. He had to nip round to the liquor store for more red wine and champagne at one stage, because the oldies were celebrating more happily than I'd catered for.

A reporter came from the newspaper to take Great-Uncle Gordon's photo and get his story. Wasn't that nice? But Grandpa, who'd decided to come after all, wandered off halfway through and was found peeing in Peg-down-the-road's water feature. He thought it was a toilet. Virginia and Georgia found him and brought him back. They were quite shocked – and so was Amy, because he still had his fly undone.

Uncle Robert passed out his business cards to everyone, which was embarrassing. Grandpa got hold of one and was squinting at it and shouting, 'What's it say? What's it say?' When someone told him it said Robert's a financial adviser, Grandpa yelled, 'He might be my son but I wouldn't trust him with my piggy bank!' Then he turned round and bumped into Aunt Helene and spilt his whiskey all over her dress. She shrieked and he tapped her with his walking stick and said, 'Yes, that was a waste of good whiskey, wasn't it?' It wasn't the quietest party on the block.

Virginia and Georgia spent the afternoon learning how to do tomboy stitch from Aunty May, and when I phoned Amy to see how the return trip was, she said the girls spent the whole flight stitching away. They're competing to see who can make the longest strip. Amy couldn't believe that something so simple could keep them occupied for hours. I think it proves my point that they don't need all the designer gear and expensive toys. Simple things are best.

I hope you're looking after yourself. That sheikh you met sounds a bit suspicious. He probably has a harem full of women, even if he did go to Oxford and speaks in a posh voice.

Love from Mum xxx

June 21

Attention: Lucy Findlay (Private and Confidential)

I am devastated, absolutely devastated! I simply cannot believe that Lombardi has a wife back in Italy! Just as well you did a check on the Internet – did his wife really email you their marriage certificate? It's a shame about the engagement party, but you should keep the ring, Lucy, after all he's put you through. Married men should by law be tattooed on the forehead.

I had coffee with Jane yesterday and she said, 'Lucy should sell the ring because it will bring bad luck.' I know it's a beautiful diamond, but perhaps there's something in that – it would always remind you of what happened, wouldn't it?

Would you like us to go away for a little holiday together, to cheer you up? It would be like old times. Just don't do anything foolish while you're in Sydney, will you? I know you feel embarrassed, but it's not your fault he's a two-timing pig. Phone me any time if you feel the need for a chat, okay?

Love as always, Cath

P.S. Jane has definitely had her nose refixed, don't you think? At least her eyebrows are level now.

June 23

Dear Fe

No, I am not jealous of Gaye flirting with Bob. He and I are good friends and nothing more. Anyway, I thought you didn't trust him? And now here you are worried I might be jealous.

The other day Pam said she thought Bob could be the silent type with hidden romantic depths. Gaye said, 'They're well hidden then, because he doesn't seem interested in women. Maybe he's gay.' I don't think so. I suspect he's just cautious, and he's not interested in Gaye.

I don't deny that I'd like to dress up and go out with a nice man once in a while, even though I'm still grieving for your father. Of course, no one could ever replace him, but I need to get on with life and get back my confidence with men. Bob's the only man I really talk to, and he's more like a comfortable slipper. If I'm going to get into the workforce, I need to acquaint myself with all sorts of people.

I could be uncontactable by email for a while as I'm taking Lucy on a paddle-steamer up the Murray. We both need a break away. Jane can't come as she wants to keep an eye on Bryan and make sure he doesn't do any more shoplifting.

Love from Mum xx

June 24

Dear Jane

Thanks for your email via Bryan's laptop – what a nice surprise! Here we are in the public library in Echuca. Lucy is emailing Lombardi to tell him she's suing for breach of promise, which I'm not sure is a good idea – he could have connections to the Mafia for all she knows. Personally I think she's had a lucky escape. She could have ended up a gangster's moll.

We're having a lovely time on the paddle-steamer, in between Lucy crying and phoning her sales reps on her mobile and trying to read our tea leaves. She thinks she should leave her job and start a New Age consultancy because she had a dream about being connected to a spirit guide called Marleah. She's also getting strong water-aversion feelings and is slightly queasy, which makes me wonder if she's seasick. Or should that be river-sick?

Anyway, the views are spectacular along the Murray, lots of overhanging gum trees with wonderful twisted trunks. Beyond are green paddocks and fruit orchards. Every now and then there are little campsites and people fishing. In fact, I feel inspired to sit down in a corner and write a children's book called 'Freddy Goes Fishing'. It's very peaceful, and apart from Lucy's broken heart and queasy tummy, I think she's enjoying the trip. I certainly am. Wish you were here.

Love Cath

June 24

DEAR VIRGINIA AND GEORGIA

Wow, you've got your own computer now, and with a Net Nanny! I'm glad you had fun at the zoo sleepover, even though Dakota wet his sleeping-bag when the lion roared. And what fun it must have been for you to feed the animals the next day.

Yes, of course you can send me emails any time. That will be fun. At the moment I'm on a puddle-steamer with my friend Lucy. Don't forget to use spell-check when you email, will you? Give Dakota and Sydney a big hiss from me.

Love from Grandma xx

June 26

DEAR JANE

No, she can't be pregnant. She hasn't got a womb, remember? You were at its burial ceremony. And I don't think she's ovulating any more. Although, now I think about it, I heard on talkback that it's possible to have a menopausal baby with an egg that's been incubating in one of your tubes. Heavens, I hope that's not the case. She's too old to be pregnant, I'm sure she's just lovesick.

I'm in the Tocumwal public library: we're on our way back. Absolutely no eligible men on the paddle-steamer, they're all old and have wives with them, although they know how to kick up their heels when they have a few drinks. Lucy has finally stopped crying – she got sick of her eyes being puffy and decided she wasn't going to waste any more tears on that 'wog bastard'. So I think she's nearly over him. She's been meditating a lot. I'm reading novels and helping Lucy to bare her soul and get everything off her chest.

The weather is cold and crisp but sunny, and this is a wonderful way to see the countryside. It's quite odd, really, Fe's cruising on the Nile and I'm cruising on the Murray. Lucy says we have parallel lives. See you next week.

Love Cath

June 26

Dear Fe

Of course I haven't forgotten about your yeast infection and rash, or that you're alone in a strange country with little money and fretting for your father. But do you ever ask how I am?

You're lucky I got paid a dividend recently and can send some money as soon as I get back. Right now, as you well know, I'm in the middle of the Murray with Lucy.

Love from Mum xx

June 29

Dear Virginia and Georgia

I'm glad you liked the books I posted you. But I'm sorry you've already read them. That was a good idea of your mother's to give them to the girl next-door for her birthday.

I had fun on the paddle-steamer, but no, I didn't catch any fish. We just chugged up the river and back again.

Give yourselves and Dakota and Sydney a big hug from me.

Love from Grandma xx

June 30

Dear Amy

Yes, I know I haven't emailed you for a while, but I didn't think you liked getting too many emails at work – or is it different at the new place? And you were here in person just recently. I do always answer the girls' emails, though, I love to hear their news.

I really appreciated you flying down for Great-Uncle Gordon's birthday, as I told you over the phone. Yes, I did fumigate Fe's bedroom after you discovered whatever it was that had gone mouldy in there. And I've left the crockery in the bottom cupboards because I agree it's more efficient the way you rearranged it. I've also bought two new fan covers for the kitchen stove and the bathroom, even though the old ones were doing the job. I really was grateful for your advice and your help, Amy.

Love from your mother x

July 1

Attention: Lucy Findlay (Private and Confidential)

I guess Darwin is as good a place as any to mend a broken heart. It's so hard being a woman, isn't it? We spend half our lives worrying if we're pregnant or not, then we hit menopause and have to worry about tubal pregnancies.

Thank you for buying me a vibrator for a thank-you present, but I have to confess it's not really me. I did try it briefly but the buzzing noise put me off, and I felt sort of cheap and dirty. Don't laugh at this, but I also felt as if the ghosts were watching me, especially James, and even Grandma Potts. She was there in my subconscious telling me I'd go blind, and I couldn't relax.

I did what you suggested and borrowed a sexy video, but I felt uncomfortable watching all those gyrations. It all seemed too mechanical. I know you think your Ecstasy Plus vibrator with the revolving heads is the best $39.95 you've ever spent, but frankly I think my Evening Delight has been a waste of your money. Although I do appreciate the thought. It's a shame to waste it altogether, so would you like it? I could soak it in antiseptic before I send it.

Remember, Lucy, you're still healing, so don't leap onto another man on the rebound. It's too soon and you're too emotionally raw.

Yes, Esra is still emailing me. Fe thinks he sounds weird and she thinks Bob's a con-man. I think she has some unresolved issues about me and other men. Anyway, I feel disappointed when I open up my mail and Esra hasn't written. I look forward so much to his news. See you when you get back.

Love as always, Cath

July 3

DEAR FE

I am very disappointed that you read my email to Lucy, which was quite obviously intended for her eyes only. As soon as you read 'Lucy Findlay (Private and Confidential)', you should have deleted it or sent it back unread, or put it in the trash bin. I'm extremely embarrassed.

Mum

July 3

DEAR AMY,

No, I did not send Virginia and Georgia a dirty email. That was not me but someone posing as me. I think you need to get a new Net Nanny.

Love from your mother

July 3

No, I do not want to join your sex club. I do not want to download any video clips, either. Nor do I wish to join G-string Grannies.

Please do not contact me again.

Mrs C. Morgan

July 4

ATTENTION: LUCY FINDLAY (PRIVATE AND CONFIDENTIAL)

I keep getting such awful emails. How do these people know I'm lonely? Well, I'm not really lonely, not as bad as I was before. I'm just occasionally lonely. I know I was a bit dependent on James, so I think I'm doing quite well, really, getting out and about and learning to cope with my new life.

Did Jane tell you that Bryan's been selling illegal substances by email? She discovered it when she was using his computer to email me. He's lucky the police didn't get onto it or he'd be in even more trouble. Poor Jane, she's putting on a brave face about her marriage and her wayward son. How are you going, my dearest friend? I hope everything is fine at your end.

Gaye, Pam and I offered to help Bob set up his new office, but he's hired Initially Interiors, which is quite a trendy company. They're expensive, but they'll do a top-class job. Bob said the whole building needs an up-market image if he's to attract a good clientele in his office and good tenants in the others, which makes sense.

There was a write-up in the paper about Initially Interiors. They do 'themed workplaces'. Bob's theme is dove and slate-grey and pale green, with chrome and silver and glass, which is apparently restful. Bob said they wanted to do baby-pink and pale blue in his office, to make it different, but he told them he was running a financial-planning service not a family-planning service.

Nothing from Esra.

Love as always, Cath

July 7

DEAR FE

No, I'm not angry with you. It was my mistake, sending you that email to Lucy in the first place.

I don't know how I managed to do that – there must be gremlins in the computer. It somehow went to Virginia and Georgia too, and you can imagine Amy's reaction. Now I'm being pestered by weirdos trying to sell me things.

I confess I have been worried – I thought you might

have been disgusted by my conversation with Lucy. You probably don't think mothers are supposed to talk about such things, but I'm a woman and I have a woman's needs and feelings. In fact, I've come to realise that I have many different facets to my life – I'm a mother, a widow, a grandmother, a daughter, a friend . . . I'd never really thought about it like that before.

Of course, when I write to you I'm your mother. I worry about you. It probably drives you crazy, as my mother used to when she worried about me, but I can't help it. One day, when you're a mother yourself, you'll understand. I'll always love you and worry about you, even when my emails are short and it might sound like I don't.

I forgot that you'd said you were going down to Aswan with the Australian guy you met, then back to Luxor on the Nile and then to Cairo by train. The photos you took with David's camera arrived in yesterday's post. The scenery from the felukah looks amazing, desert on one riverbank and lush tropical gardens on the other. So you're finally leaving Egypt and heading for Asia, but not with David because he's coming back to Australia? That's a shame, because he seemed nice and sensible. Email me immediately you arrive in Thailand, won't you?

Love from Mum xx

July 10

Dear Fe

The news here is a mixed bag, good and bad. Your grandpa got worse and we've had to put him in a home (a sort of holding pattern) until he's assessed. So Grandma has come to live with me for a while. Uncle Robert and Aunt Helene couldn't take her because of all their stairs, and of course Aunt Helene worries about her expensive carpets and furniture. (And just between you and me, your grandma doesn't want to go there.) She isn't really incontinent, like your grandpa is, she just leaks a little bit occasionally, so I've put a plastic sheet on her chair, and an old towel.

Poor thing, she's fretting for Grandpa and is very miserable, and of course he's fretting for her. I'm hoping this will be only temporary, and that with some medication he'll be able to come home, as I'm a bit worn out going up to collect the mail and feed the cat and check on the house.

Virginia has to have bands on her teeth, and Georgia won another silver medal at jazz ballet. Dakota is finally learning to wee standing up, except that he demands to 'go now', which can be awkward. Apparently he stood on the seat and peed out the window onto a lady in an open-top sports car, and Amy received a warning from the bus company. I think the modern generation is too lax with toilet training. Both you and Amy were fully trained by twelve months. Amy thinks children have rights, so Dakota has the right to pee when he wants to. When I asked her, 'What about the rights of the driver in the sports car?', I don't think she was too pleased.

Lucy has got over Lombardi fairly quickly. She's always been keen on men, as you probably know, whereas I've been emotionally dry since your father died and will probably stay that way. Women can be best friends and still have different views on life and how to live it, don't you think?

Yesterday I pop-riveted the roof where it had come loose. And did I tell you that Jane, Gaye, Pam and I have just joined a book club, to try to broaden our minds? The other women in the club are avid readers and they all have uni degrees, so sometimes I'm a bit nervous about voicing an opinion. But when we were discussing the first book, *My Mother, My Child*, I said I thought that the daughter was being made to pay emotionally, socially and financially because she was an unwanted and unplanned baby who put a stop to her immature mother's own emotional, social and financial life, and they all looked quite impressed. I'm reading *Field of Onions* at the moment. I must say it's hard going, too much description about onions for my liking. Still, must keep the brain active.

I think I told you that Gaye and I finished the water feature. We got an electrician to connect it, and Pam, who's quite good with electrical things, put in the cable for the garden lights, which anyone can legally do. Bob was going to do it, but he's in Sydney because his father is dying of a brain tumour, which is a terrible way to go.

Now it's winter I don't have to water the garden, thank goodness, but Gaye says she'll install a pop-up system for me, which will be a great time-saver in the summer. Apparently there's a very intelligent model that knows not to come on if it's raining.

Take care of yourself.

Love from Mum xxx

P.S. Don't forget to wear lots of insect repellent in Asia. The mozzies carry malaria and swamp fevers.

July 10

ATTENTION: LUCY FINDLAY (PRIVATE AND CONFIDENTIAL)

Fe is now flying to Asia. Coincidentally, Esra tells me he intends going to Thailand next in search of some lost tombs. He does such exciting things. Just between you and me, I'm quite fascinated by him. I've never known anyone like him before – not that I actually know him well, but perhaps I will one day. Did I tell you he's an archaeologist as well as an explorer? His life all sounds too amazing to be true, but underneath all his bravado I think he's lonely.

When I told Bob about Esra he said Esra sounds like a con-man. I wonder what he thinks he's conning me out of? And Esra's world seems so exciting, whereas mine is so mundane. My emails are all about lamb roasts, walking the dog, handywoman and SPUDS classes, looking after Mum and Dad, and news about the grandchildren . . . Hardly exotic, is it? I can't even get a part-time job.

You'll be pleased to hear that my social life is improving marginally, though. Gaye arranged for us to go to a dinner run by Separated Creams, as you suggested. I wish you could have come along too, but of course you were in Sydney. Pam's just not interested at all, she's quite happy with Mow.

Anyway, we went to the sales and bought new outfits. (Bob said I should spend some money on myself for a change, as I'm not that impoverished.) I bought a blue dress. Gaye thinks it brings out the colour of my eyes, but as I said, 'Only if I don't have my reading glasses on.'

We worked out that she can borrow my dress because it's loose-fitting, and I can borrow her new tangello jacket if I don't do up the front buttons, me being double C now, thanks to the extra oestrogen, and her being a B.

It's a real nuisance being a double C. I've only bought two cheap new bras in case I go back to my normal size. I keep knocking into things. It's also a nuisance remembering to take my reading glasses everywhere. You can always tell women our age, even if they've had a face-lift, because they're in the supermarket holding items at arm's length and squinting at the labels.

I was talking to Gaye about this and she said, 'What you need is multiples. I have twelve pairs scattered round the house, a stronger pair near the phone so I can read the phone book, and more in my handbag and car.' I said, 'That must've cost you a small fortune,' and she said, 'No, five dollars a pair at Cheap Chucks Superbarn.' I was horrified, and told her she'd ruin her eyes with cheap glasses, and she said that her eye doctor told her they're fine if you have no other eye problems. He even dragged out his own pair of Cheap Chucks to show her. So, seeing as I'm always losing my one pair, I think I'll buy the cheapies for round the house and use my good pair for proper reading.

July 10

ATTENTION: LUCY FINDLAY (PRIVATE AND CONFIDENTIAL)

Sorry, I pressed Send by mistake.

Back to the dinner. Unfortunately there was no one there who appealed to me or to Gaye. We've decided we're too fussy. But I did meet Paul Placebo (not sure how to spell that) at dinner, that rich alcoholic you've talked about. I must say though he's the same age as us, he looks ninety. He seemed interested in me, but I don't think he's had a bath since Christmas, when he went to visit his aunt in Double Bay. Didn't you say that she finances his lifestyle? He rolled up his trouser legs to show me his pure silk Eros and cherub socks, and showers of dried skin fell onto the carpet. If he's an example of rich and eligible, forget it!

Thought you might like these cute sayings from the Internet that Amy sent me – opinions of children about marriage:

> *How do you find someone to marry?*
>
> No person really decides before they grow up who they're going to marry. God decides it all way before, and you get to find out later who you're stuck with.
>
> Kirsten, age 10

How can a stranger tell if two people are married?

You might have to guess, based on whether they seem to be yelling at the same kids.

Derrick, age 8

Is it better to be single or married?

I don't know which is better, but I'll tell you one thing. I'm never going to have sex with my wife. I don't want to be all grossed out.

Theodore, age 8

There were lots more. Talk about out of the mouth of babes . . . I think I'll stay single. Really. I mean, after Lombardi how can you ever trust a man again? Although there must be heaps of nice ones out there somewhere.

Jane seems to be getting very depressed. I'm sure now that the plastic surgery was a desperate attempt to make Derek fall in love with her again, but it didn't work. She said her doctor has suggested antidepressants. I feel a bit down myself at the moment, so hope I won't be pressured into taking antidepressants.

Although I think it's not so much depression as exhaustion. I'm finding it harder going with Dad in the nursing home. He's been assessed by a team of geriatric specialists organised by Robert and Helene, and they've said he needs 24-hour care. Predictably, Robert wants to put him in a nursing home permanently, sell the house, and 'use some of the money to put up a little granny flat for Mum in my backyard'. Or else put her in care too.

Poor Dad keeps escaping from the home to find Mum. He's worked out the security-pad code (he was always good with figures) and so far he's hitchhiked with a bunch of surfies, caught a bus going the wrong way, and hidden in a delivery van. Last time he hailed a taxi and offered the driver a free grease and oil to take him home. The driver called the police and they took him back for the umpteenth time. They have been very understanding, but I guess even they have their limits. I drive Mum to see him every afternoon and they just sit holding hands and crying. It's so sad.

Mind you, it's a lovely nursing home. Nice roses, and they use a vanilla air-freshener so it doesn't have that awful pine-over-urine smell. Sorry to go on, Lucy, but I feel very distressed and no one seems to understand. Jane says a nursing home is the best place for both of them, and of course so do Robert and Helene. I know the care is good, but all those old folk in there seem to have given up hope. They're curled up in their beds waiting to die. It just seems cruel.

Guess we'll all be like that one day. Old and feeble. Let's make a pact: you don't let my kids put me in a nursing home, and I don't let Rohan and Tibby put you in one either. Though I don't think you need to worry about Rohan, seeing he's in the UK with Barry. And as for Tibby, I've always thought it was sad the way she distanced herself from you. It was hardly your fault when that dreadful boyfriend you had tried to come on to her that time, and you did give him the flick immediately. When she came to your womb-burying ceremony I thought I could see a bond re-forming. It was a shame she had to leave so soon afterwards. When she gets older she'll realise how important her mother is. After all, you only ever have one mother.

Must go, I need to get my own mother into the bath.

Love as always, Cath

July 13

ATTENTION: LUCY FINDLAY (PRIVATE AND CONFIDENTIAL)

Dreadful news! Jane broke down halfway through the book club, bawling her eyes out. It turns out Bryan is a drug addict. He got caught doing a break-and-enter and it seems he's been stealing to feed his heroin habit. And there's worse, though I don't know if Jane knows about this or not. Derek was seen holding hands over a table at that new restaurant, Symphony – with a very good-looking man! I'm not sure whether, as her best friends, we should tell her or let her find out for herself. What do you think?

Gaye says Jane's in too fragile a space at the moment. Pam thinks it's better to tell her and get it out in the open, then she'll know what she's up against. But what if they were just shaking hands over a business deal or something? I think we need more proof.

The doctor's given Dad some new medication, so he's not so restless, but I can tell he's still deeply unhappy. Bob is coming around to play pontoon with Mum and cheer her up.

Love as always, Cath

July 15

Dear Fe

I was very relieved to hear you got to Bangkok safely and that you're doing the five-day tour with a reliable travel group. It sounds more cultural than all that beer and partying. Though I do understand that by the time you left Egypt you were all tombed out and swimming in the Nile had lost its appeal.

Oh – can't chat now, someone's at the door.

Love from Mum xx

July 16

DEAR FE

Sorry to rush off yesterday, but it turned out to be Grandpa ringing the doorbell. He'd escaped from the nursing home again. He climbed out the bathroom window and gave a kid in the street ten dollars to borrow his mountain bike. He'd worked out that Grandma's staying here. I made him a nice cuppa and they watched Jerry Springer together. Then I gave them both some vegie soup, and thick chicken-and-salad sandwiches with lots of beetroot and grated carrot before I phoned the nursing home to say I was returning him. He was quite good in the car because Grandma came with us and she has a calming effect on him.

It's becoming quite nerve-racking, wondering what will happen next time he escapes. He could be hit by a car, or some lout could bash him up. But I mustn't dwell on negative thoughts . . .

Have you heard from Virginia and Georgia? Georgia got an A+ for her assignment on Egypt, thanks to you emailing her so much information, and Virginia has gone up a grade in netball. Dakota can finally pee straight. And into the toilet. Amy's put a ping-pong ball in the bowl so he has something to aim at, and she's put a progress chart on the wall. He gets a gold star every time he hits the ball. Sydney's had an ear infection again.

I've had to cut down on SPUDS due to your grandma staying here. Marcus seemed quite disappointed when I told him I couldn't come to psychology for a while. He suggested we meet for a coffee and go over the classes I miss. I told him that'd be lovely but I just haven't the time right now.

I'm still managing to get to handywoman classes because Peg-down-the-road comes to sit with Mum. They've always got on well and they chat about recipes and the good old days. Grandma can get around the house quite easily, but I worry she'll trip. That would be the last gasp, Grandma with a broken hip.

Love from Mum xx

July 16

ATTENTION: LUCY FINDLAY (PRIVATE AND CONFIDENTIAL)

I am so upset! I feel used and stupid! Esra's *wife* emailed me and told me he's an out-of-work alcoholic and a 'consummate liar', and she's working day and night to keep them both. She asked if I could 'please leave him alone'. I was so shocked I can't describe it.

Of course, I immediately emailed back and apologised to her. I'd never have kept writing if I'd known he was married. Although it was really only harmless flirting, nothing serious. I just can't believe I could be that gullible. It's made me even more nervous of men.

Really – first Lombardi and now Esra. Are all men liars? Lately I just feel like sitting in a corner and bawling. There's too much going on, I can't cope. There's the getting-over-James thing, the Fe thing, the Amy thing, the Jane thing, the not-enough-money thing, the social-life thing, the new-man thing, and the biggest – Mum and Dad. Sometimes I think it'd be easier if they weren't here, and then I feel terribly guilty for thinking that.

Why am I being such a selfish cow? I hate seeing them old and feeble. I love them and I don't want them to die. It's just that the constant worry is wearing me out.

Love as always, Cath

July 18

DEAR AMY

Thanks for your call. I'd been telling Fe about Dakota and the ping-pong ball. I wonder if that would work with your grandpa? The nursing home says he seems to have trouble aiming.

When you think about it, old people regress to being as helpless as babies. They lose their teeth, so they're all gummy, they lose their balance and stagger like a toddler, they lose control over their bladders and bowels and have to wear adult nappies. I suppose we should be grateful that the journey in between is more pleasant. I think I've become quite philosophical since I've been in the book club.

Oh, Grandma says next time one of the children has an earache, try olive oil and wrapping their head in a flannel scarf. She says it's an old remedy.

Love from your mother x

July 22

ATTENTION: LUCY FINDLAY (PRIVATE AND CONFIDENTIAL)

Jane came round the other day for coffee and said she feels like having a complete nervous breakdown, only she doesn't have time. She found a note in Derek's jacket signed 'Love, Nutsy'. I know you're going to say he deliberately left it there for her to find because that's what men do when they want it out in the open, but I'm not so sure.

Of course, I didn't say anything about the rumour of him holding hands with a man, but Jane says she's 'refusing him his marital rights' and has moved into Bryan's bedroom. (Bryan's not using it, as he's in rehab.) I didn't like to point out that Derek obviously isn't interested in marital rights, seeing as she's told me they haven't had sex for months. Poor Jane, I do feel so sorry for her. But she's strong and she'll survive this crisis. We all do, in the end, I suppose.

Dad seems to have given up running away for the time being, thank goodness, but now he's sleepwalking at night into ladies' bedrooms.

Keep me posted when you go to Broome for the weekend. That sounds exciting. I'm too busy looking after Mum at the moment to have a life.

Love as always, Cath

July 22

Dear Fe

Who is this BJ person from Belgium that you met on the bus to Kanchanaburi? Are they a girl or a boy?

No, I'm not going to have coffee or anything else with Marcus Candover. I'd feel too nervous to even think about getting involved with a psychologist, even a gorgeous-looking one. He'd be forever ferreting around in my feelings and analysing them.

No, I haven't applied for any more part-time jobs, as it's a full-time job looking after Grandma here and looking after her house and garden as well as my own. Yes, I know I could get some services in to help, but I don't want to do that because it will look like I can't cope, and Grandma would feel bad. Then again, I'm getting to the stage where I can't keep doing this without help.

Bob said he'd organise some services, that I only have to say the word. He says Grandma should be seeing a physio, and that I should get a gardener for her house and someone to water the pot-plants and take care of the mail and all those little jobs.

Speaking of Bob, no, he hasn't bought any more buildings or businesses that I know of. I hope that wasn't a hint of sarcasm I detected?

Must go, sorry my emails are so short these days.

Love from Mum xx

July 23

DEAR AMY

I'm glad you appreciated Grandma's old earache remedy. Since she's been living with me, we've been talking about children a lot more. You know, whenever I've suggested old remedies to you in the past, like teething jelly, you've pooh-poohed the idea and given the children modern medicine. You seem to have studied all the psychology books, so I haven't volunteered too much information. My opinions differ from yours, so I thought it best not to interfere, but since you ask, I used to give you girls vitamin C drops and you never caught colds. Grandma used to dose us with cod-liver oil for colds and tie a bag of camphor round our necks to ward off germs. Some of the old ways are good and some have been superseded, so I guess the best thing to do is try both and see what works.

I know you think I worry about Fe too much and that I've favoured her over you. That's just not so. Yes, I've always worried about her and I still do, because she's so impetuous and headstrong and wilful, and she needs protecting from herself, whereas you were always so sensible and smart and reliable. You've grown up to be a remarkable woman, Amy, and I'm very proud of you, even though you intimidate me sometimes with your attitudes to this and that. I know it's probably silly, but I feel I don't measure up to your standards, which is why I tend to withdraw myself emotionally from you.

There, I've said it. I hope you won't take this the wrong way. You're my daughter and I love you dearly and always will, but it's a different love to the one I have for Fe, and now that you're a mother yourself I hope you can understand what I'm trying to say.

Love from your mother xx

July 23

DEAR FE

I loved the jpeg of you sitting on that huge coconut under a palm tree. The scenery is absolutely lovely, all those blue lagoons and islands. And your view from the hotel balcony is beautiful. If you must go scuba-diving, be careful not to cut yourself on the coral – apparently a coral cut can take a long time to heal.

All right, I promise I'll ask Bob to organise some home help and a physio for your grandma. I promise.

Love from Mum xx

July 23

DEAR AMY

I'm so glad I didn't upset you with my frankness. It was hard to have a conversation with us both crying, but maybe this will bring us closer together. I hope so.

Lots of love from Mum x

July 26

DEAR FE

Thanks for the map. It's good to know where you've been and where you're going. I'm amazed at how many airports there are in Laos, and yet it's a very small country. And I loved the photos of the temples and shrines and people riding bicycles over rivers.

The doctors are thinking of moving Grandpa to a single-sex nursing home, as the women seem to remind him of your grandma and he flirts with them.

I'm finding Grandma good company, even though

she mostly watches daytime TV when she's not visiting Grandpa. I have to schedule her trips to see him around her favourite shows, and that it can be quite a juggle.

I did as I promised and asked for help, so now we have a lot of people with clipboards visiting – Aged Care, Geriatric Services, Respite Services, Mobility Services, and so on. I keep reading in the papers that there aren't enough of these services for the elderly. That's probably because they're all here seeing your grandma. Though I assume that things will calm down once all the assessing is over. It is good to see the physio person working on Grandma, and they've also organised for her to go to hydrotherapy three times a week. Mobility Services will come and get her. Grandma's always loved the water, so she's quite excited.

Bob took me to dinner in Melbourne the other night. A Respite person sat with Grandma and we went to the Flower Drum, which has the best food I've ever eaten. I've always wanted to go there, but it was too expensive. We had the banquet for two – shrimps and prawns and lobster and chicken and all sorts of delicious dishes – and the most superb wine. Bob's offered me a part-time job looking after the plants in his new building, watering them and changing them round. There won't be a lot of time involved and I can do it when Grandma goes to hydrotherapy, so naturally I've said yes.

I've found time to strip back the varnish from an old stool and distress it, and I'm about to distress a dresser. I quite enjoy distressing things. I'm still trying to redecorate the house, but I can't do the lounge with Grandma in it, or the third bedroom either. I've managed to get some of the peeling paint off the west wall but need to borrow some trestles and a plank to do it properly. It's not hard slapping paint on a wall, and I can watch Grandma through the window while I do it.

I know you think I'm a worry-wart, but do be careful about men you meet in Asia. You never know who'll turn out to be a drug-pusher. Those dealers managed to trap Bryan, who's been well brought up in a good family. I can just hear you saying that you always thought Bryan was 'a loser', but he wouldn't have got hooked on heroin if the drug barons hadn't brought it over here in the first place. So be careful.

Love from Mum xx

July 27

Dear Amy

Yes, I got an email from Fe too. I agree she shouldn't have been visiting a religious monument in shorts, which is probably why she got spat at. And trying to take photos of monks meditating didn't seem like a very bright idea to me, either.

The transport in Laos sounds very primitive. I don't think I'm keen on her being there, even though she says it's beautiful.

I'm glad everyone is well at your end and that you're giving the children vitamin C drops. It certainly can't hurt them, can it? And I agree it's nicer chatting through your personal computer and not at work. I don't feel so tense.

Must go. Will try and phone tomorrow and see how you went with Sydney's ears.

Love from your mum xx

July 28

Dear Fe

I'm so pleased to hear that these days you're feeling more at peace with yourself when you're alone. Sometimes we need people around us, and other times we need to be alone – and being alone is different to being lonely, I think. I know I can feel lonely in a crowded shopping mall, whereas being alone, I've found, is good for one's soul.

Bob's been busy working day and night setting up his financial-planning business, leasing the other offices and running the accountancy business. Gaye and I are thinking of going to a Murder Night. I can get Brief Respite Services to mind Grandma.

No more news, I have to take Grandma to the nursing home now. Mobility Services is coming to get us. So much easier than me getting Grandma into the car, then dismantling her chair and shoving it in the back seat.

Take care.

Love from Mum xx

P.S. Can you get mozzie repellent over there?

July 28

ATTENTION: LUCY FINDLAY (PRIVATE AND CONFIDENTIAL)

Sorry I've taken so long to reply to your last email, but I've been having huge trouble with Dad. He's taken to waltzing into strange bedrooms, and then last night he walked down the street with his penis dangling out for all the world to see (there was a full moon). He told the nurses he was sleepwalking, but I'm not at all sure.

Meanwhile I've got Mum in pain here, doubled over, hardly able to move. She strained a muscle in her back in hydrotherapy. It's very up and down: on a good day she can still get around on her zimmer frame.

I know Mum worries about Dad, but she seems happy here with me. We've being chatting a lot, and I hadn't realised how much she's had to put up with over the years. Apparently Dad was quite a lad in his day. He literally swept her off her feet and they were married three months later. Statistically they should have been divorced years ago, but I suppose it shows that sometimes whirlwind relationships do last.

I do find that having Mum here has brought us closer together – two women without our men – but it will be good when Dad can go home and they can be together again. I'm finding it a bit hard-going sometimes. I think she forgets I'm grown up, and she treats me like I'm ten years old. Other times it's a total role reversal – I'm the mother and she's the child. Then there are those wonderful times when we're on an equal footing, talking about woman-things.

Please never tell anyone I find Mum hard going sometimes. Especially Fe. It sounds so mean and self-centred, but I realise I've begun to get used to living on my own.

With Mum here, instead of throwing some two-minute noodles in the microwave or poaching a couple of eggs, I have to make nourishing meals that are easily chewable, like lasagne and shepherd's pie and macaroni cheese. Mum won't eat onions because they give her colic; white bread gives her the runs; cheese binds her up; spicy stuff gives her heartburn . . . It's all too complicated.

There's a commode in her room, but she keeps leaking on the carpet. The bedroom's starting to smell like a men's urinal. I know these things are trivial in the overall scheme of things, and I feel guilty for getting annoyed, but still.

Goodness, this was supposed to be a cheerful email . . . I haven't told Jane the story about Derek being seen holding hands with a man, because she's clammed up. I think she must have heard the rumours by now. I've been wondering whether, if she doesn't want to discuss it, I should force the issue. Maybe you could phone me? When will you be back from Perth? We need to have a good talk and work out what to do.

Must go.

Love as always, Cath

July 29

DEAR VIRGINIA AND GEORGIA

Yes, your grandma is very interested in your achievements and very proud of you both, and I'm sorry I didn't send you a little reward. I've been very busy looking after your great-grandma. No, it is not true that Great-Grandpa has gone psycho. He really likes his nursing home and has made lots of new friends. I love you all very much.

Love from Grandma xx

July 31

ATTENTION: LUCY FINDLAY (PRIVATE AND CONFIDENTIAL)

I just had an email from Fe and it sounds absolutely horrendous! She's been travelling in trucks carrying twice the number of people they're supposed to, and through the Golden Triangle of all places. I don't know why she tells me these things – I'd be better off not knowing.

I know she survived the Middle East, but in this part of the world people could be trying to push drugs on her – or worse.

Your worried friend Cath

August 1

ATTENTION: LUCY FINDLAY (PRIVATE AND CONFIDENTIAL)

Yes, I know you're right. People could be pushing drugs at Fe while she's riding a pushbike down our street. As you say, it's up to her whether she takes them or not, and I can't stop her. I just have to trust her to be sensible.

Yesterday I went to the doctor and had a pap smear. That's another thing I detest – not that it's painful, but the indignity of it! But then again, if it saves lives I suppose it's worth some indignity.

I feel so high-maintenance since menopause. And more things keep happening as you get older that naturopathy can't deal with – fallen arches, allergies (milk and too much cheese or cream give me diarrhoea; in fact, I think I've developed lactose intolerance), I have rosacea on my cheek and nose, and my bladder is only hanging on by a thread. Nothing drastic, just annoying little things.

The whole health system seems to be sick, too, if you ask me. When Mum had shingles that time, her doctor couldn't come to see her because two doctors were already away from the clinic. I had to get a maxi-taxi, with her in agonising pain in her wheelchair, to take her to the surgery. Dr Carr said to call an ambulance and take her to hospital if it happens again.

I heard on talkback that GPs can't deliver babies now, in case they get sued if anything goes wrong. I think we're going backwards. Apart from Services! Once you're in the Services Loop, they won't leave you alone. I'm still being driven mad by clipboarders knocking on the door, and I can't complain to Bob because he worked so hard to get them to come in the first place when I was being halfhearted about it all.

And I certainly can't complain to Robert. Last night, he phoned Mum and told her he couldn't afford to keep paying for Dad's nursing home because some of his investments have taken a nose-dive. Mum didn't even know that he and I were each paying half of the shortfall, because I didn't want her worrying about money. Let's face it, if Robert and Helene sold their new Mercedes, which cost about a hundred thousand, and bought a Ford or a Holden, they wouldn't have a money problem. Then again, I suppose they have the right to drive whatever car they want. It's their life, not mine.

Anyway, Mum grilled me about the fees and then she said, 'Don't worry, you won't have to pay the fees for much longer.' Then she clammed up, the way she does, and wouldn't say any more on the subject. I don't know whether she thinks Dad's going to bump himself off or what.

Even more extreme – Pam's Mow arrived on her doorstep with two large suitcases. He's left home and wants to move in. Permanently.

Love as always, Cath

August 3

Dear Amy

It was very sweet of you to offer to pay some of the nursing-home fees, but I'm sure your grandparents wouldn't want you to do that. You need the money for the children's education, and anyway I can afford it at the moment, mainly thanks to Bob. If it becomes long-term I'll have to rethink the situation, but it's fine for the time being.

I've been thinking about your phone call, and about Marla wanting the girls to go and live permanently in the US. If Dwayne says she's always put her acting career first, then I'm sure she won't win if she takes him to court. And how unfair of her to email the girls calling herself their 'real mommie'. Of course Virginia, being the more outgoing, would feel tempted to go – Marla would make it sound so exciting. It doesn't surprise me that Georgia wants to stay where she feels safe and secure, with you and Dwayne and the boys in Sydney.

It's terrible for Marla to want to split up the family. I think the only thing you can do is hold your ground, get a good lawyer, and reassure the girls that they can still go over for holidays and that everyone loves them. It's no good getting in knots about it, you'll only upset the girls even more. And the boys will wonder what's going on and get upset too. Kids pick up on household tensions very easily.

So do try to be calm and positive. I'll get Lucy to send you some of her anti-anxiety pills.

Love from your mum xx

August 6

Dear Fe

Bad news from Amy. Marla has got herself a rich boyfriend and moved to Hollywood, and now she wants custody of Virginia and Georgia. Lucy says Marla only wants them with her because they're gorgeous-looking, and it's trendy for movie stars to dress their children in mother–daughter outfits and parade through Hollywood. Amy is a wreck because Virginia thinks it'd be cool to live with her erratic, selfish mother, and Georgia is terrified and says she'll chain herself to the Harbour Bridge.

Honestly, Amy has done such a good job with those girls, and I think they both love her more than they do their own mother. They hardly know Marla, she doesn't phone them that often. I know Amy and Dwayne are a bit too materialistic, and they can drive you mad with all that keeping up with the Joneses, but their way of living's nothing like what goes on in Hollywood.

Anyway, Dwayne's going to fight it. According to him she has always been a 'party animal' and a heavy smoker and drinker, and she takes amphetamines and cocaine to stay slim. It's certainly not the sort of life two young girls should be exposed to. Maybe you could call Amy and have a word. She's feeling very vulnerable at the moment.

Bob took me to a new French restaurant here that's been getting rave reviews. The portions were rather small, but tasty. Quite a number of the other diners seemed to know Bob and came over to our table to be introduced. He told me that he and a friend are going into the restaurant business, which is why he was checking this one out. The other chap is a chef, and Bob will provide the financial backing. And don't start up again about Bob stealing my money, for goodness sake! He has all sorts of business interests which do very well.

I didn't at all like your description of travelling for eighteen hours in that crowded truck with people sleeping on their backpacks. Couldn't you get a proper bus, or a plane?

And no, I can't send you any of Grandma's sleeping pills. You're not supposed to use other people's prescription drugs, you know that.

Love from Mum xx

August 7

DEAR VIRGINIA AND GEORGIA

I'm sorry I wasn't home on Sunday night when you phoned, but yes, I have heard that your mother wants you to live with her in Hollywood in her new house. It sounds exciting, but I can't tell you whether to go or not. It wouldn't be fair of me. The courts will decide, although I'm sure you'll be allowed to say what you'd prefer to do, and that will be taken into account. But it would be sad if one of you was to live in one country and one in the other, because you're such good friends as well as sisters.

So you're both getting your ears pierced and you'd like some earrings? Fancy Dakota getting a mountain bike with training wheels just because you're getting your ears pierced. Isn't he a lucky boy? I will look for some earrings and something for Dakota and Sydney too. Expect a nice surprise in the mail.

Love from Grandma xx

August 9

ATTENTION: LUCY FINDLAY (PRIVATE AND CONFIDENTIAL)

You won't believe it, but Pam is finally meeting Mrs Mow, who found out he was having an affair and kicked him out. Pam doesn't want him underfoot permanently, but she's letting him stay in the spare room until they sort it out.

She's hoping his wife will take him back. He's only been there for three days, but she says he's got crossword puzzles and newspapers spread all over the place and there are crumbs everywhere and the two suitcases contained a mountain of dirty washing. Instead of the simple meals she's used to, he wants roast dinners like he got at home. Apparently his wife wasn't the invalid he made her out to be.

But I can't believe you have a 25-year-old lover! Are you mad? You can't possibly be contemplating marriage, you've known him less than a week. I think the tea leaves have it wrong. I really think you read too much into these New Age things. The age gap's far too big, Lucy. When you're seventy he'll only be forty. I think you need to see a doctor about hormone regulation.

And you say he's got a tongue stud? What's this fad with tongue studs anyway? I just had an email trying to sell me one. It sounds revolting. I hope no one at the office reads this or you'll be a laughing stock. For goodness sake, remember your age.

Love as always, Cath

August 10

ATTENTION: LUCY FINDLAY (PRIVATE AND CONFIDENTIAL)

What do you mean, I need a good lay? I'm not the sex maniac – you are. I happen to be perfectly content with my life, thank you. I do not want to 'bonk Bob', as you so delicately put it. I don't even have time for a relationship right now, as you well know.

What are doing to yourself? The idea of a butterfly tattoo on your buttocks is just plain stupid. When you get old and wrinkly it will look like a decayed fruit bat. This guy Brad's not in love and neither are you. It's lust. Next thing you'll be on the phone crying your eyes out and telling me he's gone off with some eighteen-year-old. You deserve better.

Love as always, Cath

August 11

ATTENTION: LUCY FINDLAY (PRIVATE AND CONFIDENTIAL)

Well, if your best friend won't tell it to you straight, who will? What's got into you? That boy must have bonked you till your brains leaked out of your private parts, along with everything else. Just don't expect me to be here to pick up the pieces when he drops you. You might think it's cute to have a toy boy, but I think thirty years is a ridiculous age difference, and he has some sick ideas about lovemaking. You're playing with fire.

Love as always, Cath

August 12

DEAR JANE

I'm glad Bryan's new job is going so well. You must be very proud of him, giving up you-know-what (I'm not game to write it or someone will try to sell me some).

I hope things are better between you and Derek. Don't despair, it might be just a passing phase.

Can you have lunch with Lucy and me on Saturday? We all need to catch up. It's harder for me to get out with my mother living here, so can you confirm and I'll get Brief Respite.

Love, Cath

August 13

Dear Fe

So you're now in Vietnam? I must say it sounds more like my cup of tea – all those lovely pastries and breads. And very French. At least you're not trucking around the countryside. The mini-buses sound much better. And the Mekong Delta bicycle tour sounds interesting. I think I'd like Vietnam, though I don't think I could cope with all that cycling.

On the home front, a place has been found for Grandpa at the Charles Danville Nursing Home and he'll be moving on Tuesday. But he's got it into his head that they make porn movies there, and that he'll be beaten with whips and chained to the bed. I think he must have watched a porn video one night when he wasn't nocturnally wandering, and it's affected him.

Uncle Robert actually drove down from Melbourne (Aunt Helene didn't come) so we could check out the nursing home together. It's very clean and tidy, with men sitting neatly in rows watching TV. Grandpa will have his own room. Uncle Robert wanted to put him in a room with three others so that he'd have company – but of course that'd also be cheaper. I think your uncle is worried his inheritance is disappearing. A private room isn't cheap, but that's what both Grandpa and your grandma want, and after all it's their money.

Speaking of money, you haven't mentioned it for a while. Have you got enough? Email some photos when you can. I always enjoy seeing where you've been.

The Aged Care people say that Grandma's house needs railings and a modified shower and a wheelchair ramp. It will cost about three-and-a-half-thousand dollars, and they say she can't go back home without them. And she can't stay here without them, either. Can the government dictate like this? After all, it's not their home, is it? Grandma's told them to leave her alone, but the fact is that I can't shower her without help. I feel really frustrated and angry about all this. It makes you realise how vulnerable you are when you get old and frail.

Anyway, I'm sure that with Pam and Gaye's help, I

could build an access ramp with handrails for a fraction of the cost the clipboard people quoted. They showed me a plan and I tell you it's more detailed than the Westgate Bridge. You could drive an armoured tank up it, it's so strong. Bob thinks it's a nudge-nudge, wink-wink deal, and some clipboarder's brother-in-law is probably in the ramp-building business.

I must go and get ready for the book club. I'm actually leaving Grandma on her own for an hour because she's convinced that the last Brief Respite person was casing the joint. I think some of Grandpa's obsessions have rubbed off on her. Or it's too much TV. Anyway, she'll have the mobile beside her with my number and I can be home in a flash if I have to, since I'll be just around the corner. A pity I haven't had time to read the book properly.

Take care of yourself, dear.

Love from Mum xx

August 19

ATTENTION: LUCY FINDLAY (PRIVATE AND CONFIDENTIAL)

It was lovely to see you for lunch, but a shame Jane didn't open up more. I knew she'd be in denial about Derek, but still it was better to get it out in the open, even if she did get a bit upset. I've phoned her a few times but she's always engaged. I know she went shopping in Melbourne with Gaye – they seem to be getting along well.

We've had a terrible time of it with Dad. He was moved kicking and screaming to the Charles Danville Home and had to be given a tranquillising injection. He arrived quiet and subdued, but keeps barricading himself in his room with his chest of drawers against the door. I don't know why – he hasn't got anything to fear from the other men. Talk about walking zombies.

This place isn't as good as I thought. On the surface everything looks fine, as it did when Robert and I checked it out, but now I think the inmates are all doped up. I'm very worried about Dad.

Mum's no fool either. When we visited she looked around, pursed her lips and said, 'He's not staying in this place.' I know her – she's hatching something, but she won't confide in me.

I'm about to start constructing the wheelchair ramp, as per the specifications. Bob's helping me dig the holes, and if this one works out I'll build one at Mum and Dad's house too. I figure that even if she goes home she'll still come here to visit. I really like working with wood. Maybe

I should start a company that builds wheelchair ramps at a low price.

Gaye wants to try another dinner party, this time through a place called Heart to Heart. You pay $120 and you wine and dine with eight other singles, who are selected through a computer-compatibility test. To be perfectly frank, the extra testosterone the doctor has put me on has revived my libido and I've started to get some, you know, feelings. But I'm too scared to have a sexual relationship, even if I find a nice man. What if I've seized up from non-use? Strictly between you and me, James wasn't exactly a sexual athlete once he turned fifty. In fact he was a bit of a flop. But we never discussed it, really, because I didn't want to upset him. And don't dare send me back that vibrator. I just can't use it and that's that.

Pam met Mrs Mow and it turns out she's very nice. Pam was furious when she learned that Mow was still sleeping with his wife after all. She heaved his suitcases onto the front lawn and told him she never wanted to see him again. He phoned later saying his wife wouldn't have him back either. Pam told him that was too bad and he shouldn't have lied to them. She says she could never trust him again. She has a very strong moral fibre.

Love as always, Cath

August 20

Dear Fe

The main news here is that Grandpa has settled into his new room at Charles Danville. But he's still a worry, as he thinks people are out to attack him. I think he's a bit scared in that new environment.

Central Vietnam sounds very cultural. Thanks for the jpegs. You know how you said in your last email that now and then you get homesick pangs and feel vulnerable – well, that's to be expected. I feel the same occasionally. I don't mean homesick, of course, because I am home, but that lost, bereft sort of feeling comes upon me sometimes. I find that having a cup of tea and reading a book or watching something lighthearted on TV takes my mind off it.

I'm glad you appreciated the money I put in your account, but I thought you'd be coming straight home after Vietnam and now you're planning to fly to Japan. I'm pleased you're not going alone, but how can Sharon and Suzie be close friends if you've only just met them? And how can you meet up with Michelle when she's already come home? I'm rather confused. Michelle told her mother (who told me when I met her in the supermarket) that hostessing is a hard job. She had to be nice to rich Japanese men and one old guy dribbled on her hand, but at least there's no sex involved. I hope you're not contemplating hostessing for money.

Yes, Grandma is still here. Must go, I'm building that ramp for her.

Love from Mum xx

August 26

ATTENTION: LUCY FINDLAY (PRIVATE AND CONFIDENTIAL)

Sorry I've been off-line. Mum accidentally disconnected the modem by wheeling over the cable and I didn't notice. I just thought I was having a drought, email-wise. I was going to phone you, but I've lost your new mobile number.

So Brad's quit the modelling job and is moving in with you? Handy for him that you'll be able to keep him till he gets another job. Come on, Lucy, I know I said it wouldn't last and here you are still together, but it sounds very one-sided in the financial department. Maybe the feng shui isn't paying off, and moving the mirror to the front of the hall to attract universal love and light just hasn't worked. Anyway, it's your life, not mine, but please don't let Brad rip you off.

Gaye and I are going to our Heart to Heart dinner on Friday night. She calls it Fart to Fart because she thinks there'll just be a bunch of old farts there. I'm wearing that black dress with the spaghetti straps you lent me – maybe it'll give me some confidence. I might have a problem with the visible panty line, though. I know you wear G-strings but I don't like them. My regular Cottontails are a bit bulky, so perhaps I'd better buy some new knickers. I'll let you know what happens.

Love as always, Cath

August 26

Dear Fe

An all-over massage with coconut oil for three dollars sounds like a good deal. And prawns and mangoes for a couple of dollars sounds divine (that's Jane's new word – divine).

Speaking of Jane, I have some news that will surprise and shock you – she's found out that Derek is having an affair with a man. I'm not sure who he is, but he's a local person. Jane suspected something was going on, but when Derek finally confessed it came as a huge shock to discover it was a man and not a woman. And Bryan is back on drugs.

Poor Jane. She's absolutely shattered, and feels she's somehow been cheated by them both. I met her for a quick lunch last week and she seems very depressed. She shredded five paper napkins while we were talking and her eyes kept filling with tears. It makes me feel helpless. She used to be so serene. I just don't know what to do.

Lucy and I are trying to help her as much as we can, but this week she doesn't want to see anyone and is keeping to herself. I went round with some biscuits, but she wouldn't even answer the door. Gaye seems to be having more luck talking to her – they've become quite close – so at least there's someone she can confide in. Jane told Gaye that she feels she could compete with another woman, but not with a man. I've heard on talkback that a lot of women feel like that.

Grandpa has come out of his room at last. Now he spends his time arguing politics and current affairs with the other men. But Grandma is still worried about him. She says that if he keeps this up someone will punch him on the nose. It's sad that at her time of life Grandma has these worries. At the other place she was worried about him chasing other women and now she's worried he'll do something totally out of character, like turn Liberal. That would mean the Waterside Workers Union (I think it's called the Stevedores now) wouldn't give him a guard of honour at his funeral. They do that for all their shop stewards, you know.

On a more cheerful note, I'm going to a couples dinner party with Gaye tomorrow night and Lucy has lent me a dress. I don't really feel like going, I have to force myself, but I know I have to get on with life.

By the way, I found out why Marcus Candover seemed interested in me – it wasn't my scintillating personality or curvy shape, it was because he's doing a PhD on grieving and death.

Love from Mum xx

August 27

ATTENTION: LUCY FINDLAY (PRIVATE AND CONFIDENTIAL)

I just don't know quite what to do about Mum and Dad. I feel a bit down at the moment with all the worry. I know Fe couldn't do anything to change the situation even if she were here, but I think I'd feel a bit more . . . well, not so alone and helpless, and worn out with all the responsibility. Robert had the nerve to say to me, 'Really, Cath, I don't see why you're complaining about feeling tired. All you have to do is feed Mum and visit the nursing home. What's your problem?'

I know you've always disliked Robert, ever since he tied your pigtails together when we were in grade 4. Though you retaliating by tying his bike to the railings with a chain and padlock and throwing away the key hardly endeared you to him either. But I know you understand exactly what I'm talking about.

The good news: I did meet a man at dinner! I was feeling a bit low beforehand, even though your dress and my new black knickers and bra should have cheered me up. His name is Rupert and he went to Newside Grammar, then an English university, I can't remember which one, and then into the family business.

He's just turned sixty and he's retired from the business but still holds a position on the board. He's got a reddish sort of face, cloudy brown eyes, grey hair and a bit of a tummy, but most men of sixty have, haven't they? His aftershave was nice. I was flattered when he took an interest in me, because the other women were beautifully groomed and quite sophisticated.

There were twelve people there. We had cocktails and were supposed to mingle before dinner, which I found quite tiring – having to sparkle. I was beginning to get a headache, so I stepped outside for a breath of air. Rupert followed me and out of the blue said, 'Would you do me the honour of sitting next to me at dinner?' The hostess had already arranged the seating, so he must have got it changed. I only ate two entrées and a petit four and no bread, so that my stomach wouldn't stick out. You know how I blow up when I eat. But I must have drunk too much wine, because when he asked me back to his apartment I agreed.

Anyway, he drove me to his place, a lovely apartment right on the beach front. Beautiful furnishings. At first I was embarrassed, but then he started kissing me and one thing led to another. But it all seemed a bit indecent, and I was worried he'd think my thighs were too fat or I wasn't doing it right. I didn't have an orgasm, I think I was too tense. I never had many with James anyway. Rupert kept asking, 'Was it good? Have you come yet?' I know in movies women writhe and yell and claw, but I've never been one to get too excited, let alone carry on like that, so I said, 'I'm a quiet achiever.' That seemed to please him.

But now I feel guilty! I'm not sure why. I'm a widow, I'm over twenty-one, I can do what I like. I guess I feel unfaithful to James, which is silly, I know. And I'm a mother, for God's sake. Good mothers don't do this sort of thing, do they? If Amy knew I'd gone to a strange man's apartment and had sex, she'd be absolutely disgusted. Once you've read this email, please put it in the trash bin.

Love as always, Cath

August 30

Dear Fe

We've finished the ramp – in record time – and I'm rather pleased with it. The clipboarders didn't think I could do it, but I showed them there's more to life than clipboards. I can get Grandma out to the car on her walking frame, drive her to Charles Danville and then borrow a wheelchair to wheel her down the passage. Much easier than trying to get her chair into the back of my car.

My next project is to erect a ramp at their place. I might drive your grandma there and she can watch TV while I work on it, then we could stay overnight.

I saw Jane again and she looked quite unkempt. She's very angry and she's determined to file for divorce.

Not much other news. Email me when you get to Tokyo, won't you?

Love from Mum xx

September 2

Dear Amy

Yes, I'm sorry I haven't been to Sydney for a while. I know you're finding it hard with Dwayne being overseas and this awful thing with Marla hanging over your head. I do want to visit, as I know you need support, but it's just impossible with Grandma living here and Grandpa in the nursing home.

And no, I won't put your grandmother in a home too, though you uncle and aunt keep saying I should. It would be cruel. She's happy here watching TV. And of course I have help now, so she's well looked after, but I can't leave outsiders to look after her while I jaunt off to Sydney for weeks. I love my grandchildren dearly, as you know, and I would love to babysit them while you go with Dwayne to see Marla, but I can't. I hope you understand that right now Grandma and Grandpa have to come first, and as soon as I get them settled and all the issues resolved I'll come and mind the children.

I know we're trying to get closer and we are making good progress. It's just that I can't cope with any more emotional things at the moment.

Love from your mother xx

September 3

DEAR ROBERT

What do you mean, I'm being selfish not going to Sydney to mind the children? If you're so worried about Mum, you might consider minding her while I go to Sydney. You can take her to Charles Danville every day to visit Dad and bring her back again. I am *not* putting her in a nursing home, even though you say you're willing to pay for that as well as for Dad now that your investments have surged. And I don't like hearing you talk about being 'reimbursed' when they both die. All you really want is to sell their house, but they're not ready to take that step. And Mum in a nursing home – it would break her heart to be stuck away like an old cardigan at the back of the cupboard. She's happy here with me.

Cath

September 4

ATTENTION: LUCY FINDLAY (PRIVATE AND CONFIDENTIAL)

No, I haven't heard a word from Rupert and I'm not going to phone him, even though he did give me his number. I think it was just a one-night stand – the thing I said I could never do.

At the time, in my half-drunk state, I enjoyed the attention, but I'm really not keen on seeing him again. I noticed Mum looking at me and frowning the next morning. I hope she didn't suspect anything, I'd die of embarrassment. Heavens, listen to me – I sound like an eighteen-year-old. I don't think I'll go back to Heart to Heart or Separated Creams. It's just not my scene.

I must say I don't see why you have to buy Brad designer clothes. Maybe he *will* pay you back when he gets on his feet, but it sort-of looks like you're buying his love. What's the point? I'd rather be lonely and single. Will Brad go with you to the New York conference? Gotta rush. I'm late for weight resistance.

Love as always, Cath

September 7

Dear Fe

We haven't been in touch for a week, so I have lots of news.

Thanks for letting me know where you're staying. The apartment sounds pretty crowded, with six of you sharing. Sharon and Suzie sound nice. Tokyo looks very busy. It's rather American, though, isn't it? All those pizza/hamburger places and Starbucks. But I guess there are a lot of Japanese eateries too.

You were lucky to get a waitressing job so quickly, although Tailfeathers seems a peculiar name for a Japanese restaurant. Your father and I always wanted to go to Japan, but we never got there. Remember how he used to love watching the sumo wrestling on TV? He always wanted to see it in real life. Maybe you could go and see it for him.

Bob has been to Japan and he tells me the cost of living is unbelievable. Meanwhile he's advised me to buy some more shares as they're doing well at the moment. On his advice I've reinvested what he's lent me. He won't hear of me paying him back till I'm more on my feet financially.

His business is doing really well and he has tenants in all the offices, and the new restaurant is set to open soon. He's a hard worker and has built up all his businesses from nothing. And somehow he's still managed to find time to help me build my deck and the ramps. I know you'll like him when you finally meet him.

Love from Mum xx

September 9

DEAR FE

Dramatic news: Grandpa escaped from the nursing home, aided and abetted by your grandmother. While I was at my handywoman class on Tuesday, Grandma sent the Brief Respite lady to the shops on some pretence or other, and then phoned a wheelchair-access taxi and took herself to the nursing home. She'd borrowed some of your father's clothes and had his old deerstalker cap pulled down over her eyes.

Meanwhile Grandpa had taken a male nurse's uniform from a laundry bag and hidden it in his wardrobe, and when Grandma came in he put on the uniform and wheeled her outside, round the garden and out the side gate, where she'd kept the taxi waiting. You have to admit it was clever of them! They went straight to their house and locked themselves in. We'd heard on talkback that if a person is of sound mind and body they can take responsibility for someone else, and the fact is that while your grandfather has gone a little peculiar he's not a danger to himself if he's in his own surrounds. Your grandmother had organised for someone to come and put a new lock on the gate, so he couldn't get out again even if he wanted to. And no one could get in either, until I got a locksmith to cut me a key.

When the clipboarders arrived to do an assessment, Grandma answered their questions through the security door and they've now agreed to give Meals on Wheels another go, as well as the district nursing service and additional home help. Isn't it wonderful that they're home again? As far as I'm concerned, they can stay there together in their own home for ever.

Of course, Uncle Robert and Aunt Helene are Not Pleased. They say your grandparents are risking malnutrition and poor hygiene and goodness knows what. Aunt Helene said, 'What will the neighbours think of us, letting our parents live in squalor?' And Uncle Robert said, 'The neighbours won't like having a crazy man living next to them and devaluing the neighbourhood.' Which is nonsense, because most people in their neighbourhood are old and quite a few of them are more or less mentally confused. He wants Grandpa and Grandma declared non-compis mentis. Can you believe it? But don't worry: they can't be declared non compis if they aren't. And Bob's offered to sort out their finances, so that leaves Uncle Robert out of that side of things.

Your grandmother is smart. She's asked me to buy a treadmill, so when Grandpa starts getting restless she can put him on that for a few hours. He's losing muscle tone, she says (he's eighty-three, for heavens sake!). She's going to give up hydrotherapy for the time being, till she sees how Grandpa copes. She's disgusted that when Grandpa was in the nursing home he just sat around and argued, and was doped to the eyeballs. Really, they should have exercise bikes and treadmills and maybe even weight-lifting stuff in those places. Doing nothing isn't good for you. And can you believe Grandpa has taken up knitting? A footy scarf in his club colours. So you don't have to worry about your grandparents, they're both very happy.

Once Grandma left here, I blitzed the place, aired and turned the mattress, and sent the cushion covers for dry-cleaning. I feel so much better in myself, and don't feel guilty any more about not coping as well as I should have with Grandma, and with having Grandpa in a nursing home.

Love from Mum xx

September 10

ATTENTION: LUCY FINDLAY (PRIVATE AND CONFIDENTIAL)

Really, I'm sorry to hear that Brad got in a sulk and moved in with your hairdresser because you wouldn't pay for him to go to New York. Are you okay? And to move in with *your* hairdresser – he could at least have moved in with his own. Now I suppose you'll have to find a new salon as well.

I hope that being in New York will take your mind off him. Go to as many shows as you can and enjoy yourself when you're not working. Will there be anyone interesting at the conference?

My news is that Dad and Mum are back home, which is a huge relief. It's a long story: I'll tell you next time you call. Jane and Derek are still together but in separate bedrooms. She's not as depressed as she was because the doctor put her on Prozac, but she's still a bit wobbly. I had her round to dinner the other night, and she's so disgusted with Derek. She can't understand why it took him twenty years of marriage to find out he was gay. Personally I think he was most likely doing it with men years ago. Fe says he's probably bisexual.

Gaye is doing her best to help Jane see that there's life after marriage. It's funny, isn't it, how friendships change. Some grow stronger, some wither, depending on what's happening. You and I will always be best friends, even if your Eternal Life naturopathics aren't making my breasts shrink as you promised.

Love as always, Cath

September 13

Dear Fe

This is it! You know how I've been wanting to get a job but having no luck, apart from watering Bob's office plants? And of course I didn't have the time when Grandma was here. Well, Gaye, Pam and I have decided to start up our own handywomen business. We'd been discussing it for a while, and last week Pam decided she was tired of all our talk with no action, so we're doing it!

Pam's the real motivator in the group, and she's got an unwavering belief that we can do anything if we put our minds to it. We've each discovered that it's next to impossible to get a handyman to do something for a woman living alone without charging the earth, trying to come onto her, or bullying her into extra jobs that don't need doing.

We're calling ourselves Busy Hands. Gaye will do the interior design and furnishings (making curtains, upholstering, as well as changing tap washers), I'll do the basic woodwork, and Pam will do tiling. We'll all do painting, gardening, gutter cleaning, and other odd jobs.

We're going to operate out of my house and use the spare bedroom as an office. Bob is going to help with the logistics of setting up. He's also doing our business plan, tax, wages and all those things, free of charge. I told him I must owe him something for all this, and he said, 'What are friends for?' Anyway, I can repay him later when we are up and running. Isn't it exciting?

Go, Busty Hands!

Love from Mum xx

September 19

DEAR FE

Well, how was I to know there's a worldwide chain of high-class call-girls called Busy Hands. I wouldn't want someone to associate us with *that* business, so we'll have to think of another name. I guess Bob didn't know either, because he didn't say anything. Though come to think of it he did have a bit of a smirk on his face when I told him. I thought that was just because he thought it was a bit twee.

What about Busy Nails? Busy Hammers? Busy Bees? Grey Power Girls? Put on your thinking cap, Fe, you were always good with names.

I noticed you sent your last email at six a.m. You must have turned over a new leaf to be getting up that early. Are there Internet cafés open twenty-four hours a day? Maybe you could take origami lessons or something to fill in the time when you're not waitressing? You should buy some support pantyhose. It's not good for your legs being on your feet all day, and varicose veins run in the family.

I was so pleased to hear you're going to the sumo wrestling with some business people on Saturday. Did you meet them at the restaurant? Be careful of the raw fish – you could get salmonella poisoning.

Love from Mum xx

September 20

TO BUSYHANDS@WORLDWIDE.COM

Thank you but I am not starting up a massage business in competition with Busy Hands. I am starting a handy-women business, which will in no way be confused with your own.

Sincerely

Catherine Morgan

September 21

DEAR AMY

I enjoyed our long chat on the phone and I'm glad you think our business venture is a good idea, even though it means I'll have less time to come to Sydney for visits. I'll try to come up before Christmas, even if it's only for a night. I wouldn't want the children to think their grandmother isn't interested in them. I know you liked Bob when you met him, so perhaps he could come too? He doesn't have grandchildren of his own, but he loves kids and as you saw he was really good with Virginia and Georgia at Great-Uncle Gordon's party.

But of course the best news is about Marla getting a leading role in that film being shot in Alaska and withdrawing her custody claim. That's just wonderful! You know, I had a feeling she'd change her mind. Hope to see you soon.

Love from your mum xx

September 23

DEAR FE

Another six a.m. email from you – if you're having trouble sleeping, maybe it's those futons. Lucy suggests Sleep Easy, which is made from valerian, so it's natural. Let me know if you'd like me to send you some.

I liked your suggestion of Hands On, but there's bound to be a massage company by that name too. And Hammer Heads sounds a bit like a rock band, don't you think? I thought of Working Girls, but that's got bad connotations too. I didn't realise naming a business would be so difficult.

This email is short because I'm off to take the dog for a walk, then out for lunch with Bob and the girls so he can show us the business plans he's worked out. Then I have to make a casserole for Grandpa and Grandma. Your grandpa's still not happy with Meals on Wheels. He says it's all part of a Liberal plot to destroy the waterside workers of the world.

The trouble is he wants gourmet cooking at pensioners' rates, so now they're only getting deliveries on Mondays and Thursdays and I'm making their other meals. But on the whole they're coping marvellously and I'm so pleased for them.

Love from Mum xx

September 24

ATTENTION: LUCY FINDLAY (PRIVATE AND CONFIDENTIAL)

So, how's the conference going? And what's it like in New York? I suppose you haven't had much time for sightseeing.

Amazing, you bumping into Colin Lacey. Of course

I remember him. I always thought you should've stuck with him rather than Barry. Didn't you have a huge fight and tell him to get lost, and then straightaway start going out with Barry? Anyway, what's he doing now and what does he look like? All I remember is that he had lovely thick dark Brylcreamed hair and Elvis sideburns.

It was nice of him to take you to the opera. Remember when we saw *La Bohème* in Melbourne, and we had those dreadful seats with large people in front of us and couldn't see a thing? And he just gave you a kiss on the cheek at your hotel-room door – he always treated you nicely.

Typical that you should meet him just as he was leaving New York. But lucky that he still lives over here. Then again, maybe you should forget about men for the time being and just concentrate on life in general. Allow yourself some recovery time. I'm saying this as your best friend, with your best interests at heart.

Did you know that Bryan's back in rehab again? Jane is trying to talk him into having one of those implants that stop you wanting heroin. She looks like hell on earth. I am really worried about her.

Speaking of drugs, Dr Valushi dropped my oestrogen to 10 and added more progesterone (300) because I got some spotting which turned into a full-blown period. My God, you forget what it's like when you haven't had one for years. Such a bother! I think I'd rather go off hormone replacement altogether and put up with whatever the effects are than go back to having a period every month. I didn't have a tampon or sanitary pad in the house, so I had to use an incontinence pad that Mum left behind. It felt like I was wearing a nappy. So that's what we've all got to look forward to? The good news is Dr Valushi says that with less oestrogen my breasts will reduce too.

Our business plans are forging ahead. After much discussion, we've decided to call ourselves Simply Handywomen. We thought of Busy Singles, seeing as we're all divorced or widowed, but I think the other is better. I'll see about some business cards once Bob has registered the name.

Take care of yourself.

Love as always, Cath xx

September 27

Dear Fe

Are you sure you're not suffering from insomnia, or are Japanese times back to front like the dates? Heavens, up to

30 000 yen a day, plus commission. Bob says that's about $450. If that's what waitresses get, how much would a doctor or a teacher earn? Bob wants to know if this is tax-free, because if it is he'll come over and work as a waitress himself. So will I! Are you *sure* you're not working in one of those dreadful hostess bars? Lucy says they're all run by the Mafia. And is sex involved? Because if it is, I'll be on the next plane to Tokyo and drag you home. Your father would be horrified.

Mum

September 29

DEAR AMY

No, Fe is not working as a hostess in a sleazy Japanese bar. Whatever gave you that idea? She has a perfectly respectable job at a restaurant called Tailfeathers, which serves chicken. I don't care if Dwayne did check Tailfeathers on the Internet. There are probably three or four places with that name – Japan might be a small country, but it has a lot of people and a lot of restaurants and bars.

Love from your mother x

September 30

Dear Virginia and Georgia

I'm sorry but I can't send you money for your school excursion to Fiji, as all the money I have is going into my new business. It's called Simply Handywomen.

Great-Grandma has gone back home to live with your great-grandpa. I will try to visit you all soon, or maybe you can come and visit me in the school holidays? You could get the plane and I could meet you at this end.

Love from Grandma xxx

October 4

Attention: Lucy Findlay (Private and Confidential)

Glad you had a good trip back from New York. You're probably jetlagged, but let's try to have lunch next week. Lots to catch up on.

Anyway, here's some news. You are not going to believe this. Never in a million years. Guess who Derek's lover is? Marcus Candover, my psychology teacher from SPUDS! Derek has now decided to leave Jane and move in with him. I told Pam and she said she always thought there was something about Marcus . . . Gaye said he should change his name by deed poll to Marcus Bendover.

Jane is shattered, but it would have been even worse if she'd been in the psychology class. I will not be enrolling for advanced psychology, that's for sure.

I'm afraid I'm not much good at cheering Jane up. I'm scared I'll say the wrong thing. She's a mess with a capital M, and bitter about men in general. I know this sounds awful, and karma will bite me on the backside one day for saying it, but I actually think she's nicer now that she's not so poised and perfect. Don't you dare tell her I said that! (I won't tell Gaye, she'll think I'm mean.)

I really don't know what's happening to me. I must be giving out sexual vibes. I went to pick up the samples for our business cards from the print shop, and the man at the counter started chatting to me, flirting a bit, and I was flirting back just for practice (I thought I'd forgotten how, but it's like riding a bike). Then he tried to put his arm around me! I pushed him away and told him not to be so silly, but he winked and said he was looking forward to seeing me again when he told me to come back when I'd decided which card design I wanted. I wonder if he does that to all his female customers?

Then when I got the samples home and looked at them properly, I saw he'd written 'Simple Handywomen'. But I'm not going back, I told Gaye to go – and to beware, as he's on the prowl. She said it wouldn't be a problem – if she liked him she'd take him up on his offer, and if she didn't she wouldn't. I wish I could have that casual an attitude.

Glad to hear that you've already met up with Colin for drinks and the theatre. No, I don't think he's turned gay or bi just because he's not jumping on you. He is just treating you with respect. And yes, I'm sure he's in good working order – if he has a chain of chemists' shops he'd have an endless supply of Viagra. Let yourself enjoy an old-fashioned courtship. You used to fascinate him then and you obviously still do. Just be yourself.

Now that Mum and Dad are quite happy at home and are coping well, I'm back to worrying about Fe. I just know she's working as a hostess in this Tailfeathers place, although she insists she isn't. I've been too nervous to check it out on the Internet. And I feel guilty that I don't trust her. I don't know, kids never stop being a worry. Just look at Bryan.

What do you think I should do, Lucy? Advice please.

Love as always, Cath xx

October 4

Attention: Lucy Findlay (Private and Confidential)

Oh my God, I finally did a search and found Tailfeathers in Roppongi on the Internet. It's a club with dancing girls and hostesses. I will kill Fe when I get my hands on her! How can she be so stupid? And what to do now?

Love as always, Cath xx

P.S. When Gaye went to get the business cards organised, that guy didn't make a move. In a way I was quite flattered, because she's slimmer than me.

October 5

Dear Fe

I can't believe you've been working as a hostess. *And* that you lied to me about it! Don't you know how dangerous that is? What about that British girl who was working in Tokyo as a hostess and ended up being murdered? If you needed money, I'd rather have borrowed it from the bank than have you work in one of those places. Dancing girls in feathers! Tailfeathers, indeed. Please respond immediately or I will be on the next plane to Tokyo.

Mum

October 7

ATTENTION: LUCY FINDLAY (PRIVATE AND CONFIDENTIAL)

What a shame we couldn't have lunch. I hope you get the problem in Adelaide sorted out. But we must get together soon. I need to talk to you face-to-face. I think I'm going insane! What with Fe working as a hostess, and now something else awful has happened – Jane's had a real breakdown. She's in Lonely Pines, that psychiatric place.

The strain has just been too much – even Gaye's retail therapy didn't help. I tried to be as positive as I could when I called. I told her she was in the best place possible and that they'll help her get better. She said, 'I feel like shit,' which I couldn't believe as she never swears. I promised to go and water her pot plants and feed the cat, but if she's away long-term I'll have to arrange for one of her neighbours to do it. If she lived closer to me it'd be easier, but of course she's on the other side of town, in the opposite direction to Mum and Dad.

Anyway, I took her a nice pot plant for her window-sill because you know how much she loves plants.

You just never know what's round the corner, do you?

Love as always, Cath xx

October 8

ATTENTION: LUCY FINDLAY (PRIVATE AND CONFIDENTIAL)

Okay, lunch next Wednesday at Antipasto's. It's a date.

Now, the latest news. Yesterday I bumped into Rupert outside the Rug Bazaar. He immediately apologised for not phoning – said he'd lost my number and couldn't remember my last name. Of course, he could have phoned Heart to Heart to find out, but being a man he wouldn't think to do that. I declined when he asked me out because I don't see any future in rolling about half-naked on his rug, and anyway I'm far too busy. Mind you, it was flattering to know he was still interested and I wasn't just a one-night stand. I felt quite good about that, really.

So you've been seeing more of Colin. I'm glad (for your sake) that you succeeded in seducing him and that he was very energetic – with no Viagra. (Joke: What happened to the man whose Viagra tablet got stuck in his throat? He had a stiff neck for a week.) It's great that you two are compatible in bed as well as out. And his chemist shops even stock Eternal Life! You can't get much more compatible than that. Well maybe you could, but at least you're both in the health business.

So, does he like his eggs hard-boiled or soft? It's like a new beginning, isn't it? It's strange how fate works. You could have married Colin, but you married Barry. I know you regret the wasted years without Colin, but then you wouldn't have had Rohan and Tibby. I think it was meant to be like this, and now you can live happily ever after with Colin.

Meanwhile, yes, the grandchildren are all fine, thanks. The girls keep winning medals and awards. Their talent doesn't come from my side of the family, I can tell you. I can't dance or play a musical instrument for nuts. Dakota is riding his mountain bike and Sydney is crawling everywhere, under beds and behind sofas. Amy says she wishes she could get him microchipped, like the dog, so she can find him easier.

I'll try to fly up to Sydney straight after Christmas and spend what Amy keeps calling 'quality time' with them. They suggested I go there for Christmas, but that would mean leaving Mum and Dad on their own, and anyway I've invited Bob to Christmas dinner with all the old relatives. I often feel pulled in too many directions. Sometimes I feel like a piece of old frayed knicker elastic.

Fe has come clean and admitted she's working as a hostess and saving every yen for a new car when she comes back. What could I say? I can't afford to buy her a car. She's adamant there's no sex involved, plus she's learning to speak Japanese. Apparently all she has to do is laugh at the men's jokes and flatter them and get them to buy drinks. With her looks and intelligence I'm sure she'd be a valuable asset in that business.

Anyway, I phoned her friend Michelle, who's back home with a heap of tax-free money, and she said there's definitely no sex unless you make private arrangements after hours. She said most of the girls don't, unless it's someone they really fancy, and then it's more for that reason than the money. That made me feel a bit better.

Simply Handywomen is looking good. We should be ready to start taking on jobs soon.

Jane is still in Lonely Pines and on drugs to calm her down. I popped in to see her but she just sat staring into space and didn't seem to know who I was. Her psychiatrist said this is normal. It doesn't seem normal to me, but then maybe it's just a short-term thing. Apparently Jane didn't recognise Pam or Gaye either. We need to be patient. And cross our fingers that she'll be back to her old self soon.

Love as always, Cath xx

October 10

DEAR AMY

Sorry I wasn't home when you called. I was having dinner with Bob at a new Japanese restaurant. I'm becoming quite a foodie. By the way, it's no use snapping 'Pick up, pick up, Mother' into the machine when I'm obviously not home.

I'm sorry I haven't been able to get up to Sydney, and I'm sorry I can't come for Christmas, but you know I always have the relatives over. Although this year I'm doing it at your grandparents' house because it'll be easier to move the food there than to move them here.

But I thought I'd come up for a week or so straight after Christmas. What do you think? Let me know when you've had a chance to think about it. Give my love to the children.

Love from your mother xx

October 13

ATTENTION: LUCY FINDLAY (PRIVATE AND CONFIDENTIAL)

Great to catch up with you the other day, even if briefly. I really liked that roasted pumpkin and sage roulade with Persian fetta, didn't you? That new chef is certainly doing interesting food.

Well, having said I wouldn't go out with Rupert again,

I got another phone call from him and in a weak moment I agreed to have dinner with him last night. I thought he meant dinner at a restaurant, but instead he'd arranged for it to be brought to his apartment. Nice 'posh' food. Asparagus soup, roast duck with polenta, steamed vegetables, and a coffee-meringue dessert.

Of course, he was expecting sex afterwards, which I'd anticipated, and as I was feeling mellow from the wine and he's a nice enough sort of man I was happy to give it another go. I think he must be on Viagra, because I didn't have any trouble, thank goodness. I remember James would be sometimes, well, you know, flabby, and it was such a bother to get him organised.

But frankly, Lucy, this was not at all like sex with James. All those different positions. Seems to me that nowadays a woman has to be a contortionist. What happened to the good old missionary position? I honestly don't think I can be bothered seeing him again: that dinner reinforced my belief that I'm a romantic at heart, while he admitted he has no interest in having a relationship – this was just another one-night stand for him. (Is there such a thing as a two-night stand, would you say?)

Sex with strange men is just too mechanical for me. I need to be in love, I'm a dozen-red-roses-and-chocolates girl, a moonlight-walk-along-the-beach girl. I want to be courted properly, like James did, not treated like a casing for a sausage.

Look at you and Colin. He's clearly besotted with you, but it sounds like you're enjoying the sex as well as the romance and wooing. And you *like* showing him new positions – but then, you did ballet for years and I remember how easy it was for you to do the splits. Your muscles are probably still flexible, whereas mine seized up years ago, after childbirth. That was the last time I had my legs stuck up in the air wide apart. Frankly, I think I'll retire from men, and just concentrate on work.

Love as always, Cath

October 14

Dear Fe,

Yes, I got your letter with the pamphlets on the sumo wrestlers. Your father would have enjoyed them. One day I'll come to Japan and see it all for myself. Fancy lots of the sumos being Mongolian nowadays. I didn't know that. Speaking of Mongolian, a new restaurant called the Mongolian Palace has opened in the city. Bob said we should try it, so we might go there on Friday.

Bob has admitted to me that some of the investments he and your father made didn't work out. He is accepting the blame, but I know from the correspondence in your father's files that Dad invested the money in one particular company that Bob had advised him against. So, you see, Bob actually lost money through your father's mistake, so there is absolutely nothing shonky going on. In fact, I probably owe Bob money, if the truth is known.

Love from Mum xx

October 17

DEAR FE

Yes, Virginia, Georgia, Dakota and Sydney are all fine. Maybe you could send them some Japanese things – the boys might be interested in sumo wrestling. Did I tell you I plan to go up to see them after Christmas? You'll be home by then, I hope.

I told you that poor Jane had a breakdown, didn't I? There's so much going on at the moment that I have trouble remembering who I've told what. She's in hospital doped up to the eyeballs, poor thing. She didn't even know who I was. Everything's just been too much for her.

Personally I think Derek and Marcus deserve each other. But whatever you say, I still can't understand how Derek could be married one minute and fall in love with a man the next. But it's not right of me to be so judgemental. I suppose it will all work out in the end.

Must go, I have to get ready for the book club. We are discussing *Love, Hate and Other Moments*, which I found quite complex, with many layers. I haven't been to book club for a while so I'm looking forward to it, even though Jane won't be there.

Love from Mum xx

October 18

ATTENTION: LUCY FINDLAY (PRIVATE AND CONFIDENTIAL)

Dinner at my house with Bob sounds like a lovely idea. Come around seven for drinks. Does Colin like roast beef? Or should I do lamb? And what about dessert? My apple crumble? Then again, maybe we should have a barbecue? Bob and Colin can talk men's stuff while they do the cooking and we can talk girl stuff.

Yes, a barbecue. I'll do garlic prawn kebabs and baby octopus. And some pepper steaks. And a few sausages. It doesn't matter how fancy barbecue food is, you can't beat a sausage wrapped in bread, can you? And I'll do a pasta salad and a green salad.

I think I'll wear my lime-green top and black pants. What about you?

Love as always, Cath xx

October 20

DEAR FE

Lucy and Colin and Bob and I had a barbecue here last night. It was a huge success, even though my old Webber takes an age to heat up and we didn't eat till late. I must buy one of those stainless-steel, four-burner gas ones when I have some spare cash.

Bob and Colin got on well. Of course, Lucy and I knew Colin when he had hair. Back in the sixties. He's quite bald now, and pudgier, but still really nice. He's quieter and more 'normal' than the usual men Lucy is attracted to. Let's face it, the last lot were disasters.

I wonder what would have happened if Lucy hadn't broken off with Colin first time round and married Barry? But now she's come full circle and found him again. She is very, very happy, and I am hoping that big things will come of this relationship. Colin's well-off enough to indulge her, but sensible enough not to let her get away with too much. As you know, Lucy sometimes needs a firm hand. I actually think he's the man she's desperately looked for all her life.

Thank you for the Tokyo Web-link – so many cafes and restaurants. I thought you'd be living on rice and fish and boiled noodles. It all sounds very nice, except I don't think I could eat in a place called Chunky Cafe, even if they do have the best kebabs in town. I suppose you can get meals at Tailfeathers?

I was amazed when you said how much the customers have to pay for your drinks, given they're only soft drinks, but I suppose you couldn't be drinking alcohol from eight at night till three in the morning. And it's good that they have a snack bar. Tempura sounds nice, but I wouldn't want to eat sea urchins.

Love from Mum xx

October 23

DEAR FE

Thank you for the jpegs of your apartment. I can't believe that six of you sleep in that one room, with only one toilet and shower between you, and you pay 160 000 yen per month. That's incredible – $600 a week! And you all sleep on the floor in sleeping bags. But then I guess you're making lots of money and six people divided into $600 is $100, so that's quite cheap really, isn't it?

I see you use your backpacks as room dividers. That's creative. Do you have hanging space for your clothes? It all sounds a bit primitive, but at least with six of you there you're not likely to get raped or murdered in your beds. (Not that you've got beds, of course.) I suppose that's one less thing I have to worry about.

Love from Mum xx

October 24

DEAR FE

Thanks for the new jpegs. Yes, I can see that you have some hanging space.

My big news is that Simply Handywomen has opened its doors and already we have three jobs, with seven more people interested. Pam said, 'Don't worry, we can always recruit more workers.'

Practical Pam. I've become even closer to her lately, what with Jane in Lonely Pines, Gaye trying to help Jane and also trying to sort out her sons, Lucy being with Colin, and you in Tokyo. Funny, I was talking to Pam about Lucy's new relationship the other day and she said, 'Cath, the trouble with you is you can't see what's right under your nose.' Then she wouldn't say any more. I don't know what that's supposed to mean. The only man I've got any sort of relationship with is Bob, but we're just friends.

Anyway, we're getting work quickly because we did a letter-drop in all the mail boxes in the area and our prices are very affordable, but now we're worried we'll end up with too much work. Our target is pensioners and the elderly and women living alone. Some jobs we can split between us and for some we'll go as a team. Gaye is really keen to finish her plumbing course and get her Home Plumbing Certificate. That would qualify her to do things like sign a Certificate of Compliancy.

I've been watching a program about small business on Sunday mornings, and it's been a real eye-opener. They say the first rule for success is that you have to be passionate about what you do, which we are. The second is to 'maximise sales and marketing opportunities' and not just concentrate on providing the service. So I'm now thinking of doing a small-business marketing course next year at TAFE. Me, a business person? It's a bit unbelievable, isn't it? But then again, this is the new, re-invented me. I'm finding it quite exciting.

My hormones have settled down and I seem to have a lot more energy now.

Love from Mum xx

October 26

ATTENTION: LUCY FINDLAY (PRIVATE AND CONFIDENTIAL)

I can't believe your news! You're engaged to Colin? It is very soon but, as you say, you're both in love and you're not getting any younger, so why not? So don't give that business with Lombardi another thought. Colin is a lovely man and I think you are made for each other. It's fate and it's meant to be and all that. And anyway, you're a short-time-frame kind of person.

So the ring is a big cluster of diamonds on white gold? Sounds lovely. I can't wait to see it. Pity Colin didn't know that your favourite stone is a sapphire, but you could drop a hint for your birthday, couldn't you?

I'm really very excited for you, Lucy. When is the wedding? And where? Or haven't you got that far yet? I just realised that your married name will be Lucy Lacey! Or will you keep your own name? Let's meet next week so I can admire the ring. It can't be a long lunch, though, because I'm a working girl now.

I've been to see Jane and she looks much better now

that they've reduced the drugs. I wonder if she'll be allowed out for the wedding. I don't think she could be a bridesmaid, though. It would be too much too soon. You'll certainly notice the change in her: she's lost a lot of weight and her eyes have sort of sunk into her head and her skin is pasty. Her hair has gone a bit straggly and you can see the white roots. But she's the same Jane underneath – well, she will be soon, I hope.

Simply Handywomen is keeping me busy. We've replaced some wonky cupboard doors with some Pam got cheaply at an auction and fitted perfectly. Gaye's done a fantastic job replacing some broken tiles for an old pensioner and we just have to put a final coat of paint on the wall. Gaye's also found a plumber and an electrician who will work for us at 'mates' rates'. It's amazing how everything has fallen into place.

Anyway, congratulations again. I'm so flattered that you want me to be your bridesmaid for the third time. (I'm counting Lombardi as number two because you did ask me to be your bridesmaid, even though it fell through). Third time lucky?

Rupert phoned, but I told him I've decided to become a lesbian. That should put him off.

Can't wait to see you.

Love as always, Cath xx

October 27

DEAR FE

I thought you'd enjoy this. Pam emailed it to me.

Prince Alfred was captured by the king of a neighbouring kingdom. The king planned to kill him, but instead decided to set him free if he could answer a very difficult question. Alfred would have a year to figure out the answer, after which, if he failed, he would be killed. The question: What do women really want?

This seemed an impossible question. But, since it was better than death, the young prince accepted the king's proposal. He returned home and began to poll everybody: princesses, priests, wise men, even the court jester. But no one could give him a satisfactory answer. Someone suggested that he ask the old witch, but he knew she'd demand a high price. Finally the last day of the year arrived, so Alfred had no alternative. The old witch agreed to answer his question, but he'd have to accept her price first: she wanted to marry his brother Charles!

Prince Alfred was horrified. She was hunchbacked and hideous and made obscene noises. He refused to force Charles to marry her, but Charles agreed in order to save his brother. So the witch answered Arthur's question. What a woman really wants is to be in charge of her own life.

Everyone instantly knew that the witch had uttered a great truth and that Alfred's life would be spared. And so it was.

As the honeymoon hour approached, Charles steeled himself and entered the bedroom. But what a sight awaited him! The most beautiful woman he'd ever seen lay before him. She announced that as he'd been so kind to her when she'd appeared as a witch, she would henceforth be her horrible, deformed self half the time and for the other half she would be her beautiful maiden self. Which would he want her to be during the day, and which during the night?

Charles pondered his predicament. During the day, a beautiful woman to show off to his friends, but at night, in the privacy of his home, an old witch? Or would he prefer having by day a hideous witch and by night a beautiful woman with whom to enjoy many intimate moments? Noble Charles replied that he would let her choose for herself. Upon hearing this, she announced that she would be beautiful all the time, because he had respected her enough to let her be in charge of her own life.

I think there's a moral in this somewhere. (Pam said the moral is always to respect a woman's right to be in charge of her own life, otherwise *things might get ugly!*)

Love from Mum xx

P.S. Lucy is engaged to Colin Lacey!

October 27

DEAR VIRGINIA AND GEORGIA

I am sorry I can't come and visit and take you to Luna Park because, as you know, I now have a business and I can't give myself a holiday yet. But I will definitely come and see you straight after Christmas.

What would you like for Christmas? Kisses to you and Dakota and Sydney.

Love from Grandma xxx

October 27

DEAR VIRGINIA AND GEORGIA

Regarding the presents you asked for. Diamond earrings are a little expensive. What about little gold hearts? Or maybe zodiac signs? And I'm not really happy about giving Dakota a Bazooka Blaster. I think I'll send him a big jigsaw puzzle. I also think I could send Sydney something more suitable for his age than a Rap CD.

Well done, graduating to Extension Tap classes. I was sorry to hear about Dakota's accident with his mountain bike. I do agree it was wrong of the old man to try and whack such a little boy with his walking stick, even if Dakota did run over his foot. But he probably got a big fright.

Love from Grandma xx

October 28

Dear Amy

No, I am not buying the girls diamond earrings, or Dakota a Bazooka Blaster. Or a CD for Sydney. I said I would buy hearts or zodiacs and a jigsaw puzzle.

New news: Lucy has just got engaged to Colin Lacey, an old flame. Any more news about that job Dwayne applied for?

Love from your mother xx

October 29

Attention: Lucky Findlay (Private and Confidential)

I think a summer wedding is nice on December 15th. But I am not going to wear pink taffeta shot with orange and a red bolero top. I'll look like a bloody sunset.

Okay, I've had a couple of glasses of wine, but I am mainly grumpy about pink and orange and red, and tired from working twelve hours a day. Maybe you should get someone else to be your bridesmaid.

Cath

October 30

Attention: Lucy Findlay (Private and Confidential)

I can't believe I wrote that awful email. Can you forgive me? I was feeling a bit sorry for myself, what with Jane being sick and Fe in Japan and Amy thinking I'm a slack grandmother and the grandchildren thinking I'm a money-tree, and Simply Handywomen taking up so much time and Bob in London on yet more business, and you in love and me with no one, and Dad undoing his fly in front of a clipboarder while Mum was in the shower.

Anyway, it must have been the wine – as you know, I'm the proverbial two-pot screamer. Of course I will wear rose taffeta shot with tangerine, and even a red bolero, if you want. I know I need to tone in with your hibiscus-pink dress and the mauve veil. And your tropical bouquet. I can see that since Colin has been married twice before in all-white weddings and widowed twice in all-black funerals, you'd want to steer clear of those particular colours. And I appreciate that your tea-leaf reader kept coming up with tropical tones. Is that why Colin is wearing a mauve tie?

Getting married on a beach at sunset on Daydream Island sounds just like a fairytale. I'm determined to get thinner for the wedding. I have started a new diet of pumpkin seeds, dried fruit, mountain bread with organic sundried tomato paste and low-fat goats' cheese, chopped spinach, lemon juice, and three litres of water per day. It was invented by a group of doctors in the Middle East and they say it's guaranteed to remove ten kilos in a week. Apparently all those foods have a combustible effect in the body and burn fat. It's called the Highly Combustible diet.

Anyway, my best friend, we have survived through thick and thin and I hope my drunken words haven't caused a rift between us. We've only ever had two big arguments in our lives, haven't we? The first was when I was mad keen on Hugh Wallington and you French-kissed him at a party and he dropped me for you. (Though in fact you did me a favour, because he had cold sores and it took you ages to get rid of them.) And the other time was when I gave you that walnut coffee table and you sold it. (But then the people who bought it demanded their money back when they found the table had borers. So it was pretty even, really.) But these things are minor in the overall scheme of life.

Love as always from your repentant friend, Cath xx

P.S. Just an afterthought: how did Colin's wives die?

November 1

Dear Fe

Is everything all right? I haven't heard from you for a while. Please let me know if you are okay.

Love from Mum xx

November 2

Dear Jane

I was so pleased to hear from you and to learn that the new drugs are making you feel calmer. Your psychiatrist sounds wonderful – it's great that she's helping you to move on. Are you well enough to be allowed out of Lonely Pines for a few hours? Can you come for lunch on Monday at Gregio's? Lucy will be back in Melbourne and is dying to show you her ring. I'll take some time off from Simply Handywomen, as my friendship with you two is much more important than repairing a stair railing.

Bye from Cath xx

November 2

Dear Fe

Where are you and are you all right? I've tried calling the phone numbers you gave me and all I get is a recorded message in Japanese. PLEASE ANSWER.

Love from your worried mum xx

November 2

Dear Amy

I'm truly sorry that I forgot to send the children's gifts. I have been working such long hours with Simply Handy-women I just haven't had time to get to the shops. I'll do it tomorrow and express-post them. Give my love to every-one and kisses for the kids.

Love from your mum xx

November 4

Attention: Lucy Findlay (Private and Confidential)

I know, I know. It was totally inappropriate of Jane to bring her psychiatrist to our private lunch without asking us. I really think that if Jane was in such 'emotional danger' from us, as Julie suggested, she shouldn't have left the hospital.

Wasn't it awful having our every word being analysed? I have never felt so uncomfortable in my life. What business is it of Julie's, your getting engaged after only knowing Colin for five weeks? And the way she pursed her lips when she looked at your engagement ring . . .

And what a cheek to say that she believes you have 'a serious problem' with long-term relationships. Obviously Jane has told Julie all about your past lovers, which was a total breach of trust. I know we probably do figure strongly in Jane's life, but isn't it rather poor taste to discuss private friendships with strangers like psychiatrists?

And talk about manipulating the conversation all through lunch. 'What does Jane mean to you?' How can you answer what a long and dear friendship means to you in a few sentences that you know will be analysed to pieces? I'm sure those questions were unethical. Certainly they didn't seem professional to me.

And then she started on me and the five stages of grieving. Of course I have been grieving, but I'm basically making an effort to get over it and I've moved on. I don't know what we can do about this situation except to let it run its course. I think the biggest problem is that Julie's confusing Jane with psycho-babble.

Moving on from Jane, I'm quite worried about Fe as I

haven't heard from her for a week. I phoned Michelle and she said Japan is totally safe and little kids catch trains all by themselves and you can walk the streets without getting molested. But what about the British hostess who got murdered?

Yes, I do miss Bob. He's so dependable. Every time the phone rings or there's a knock at the door I think it's him, but then I realise he's still in London. I wish he'd come back. I need some financial advice.

That's so sad about Colin's wives. A car crash and cancer. No, I wasn't thinking he might have poisoned them or something. He's too nice. I'm glad you've brought some happiness into his life.

Anyway, I enjoyed our lunch despite the Julie fiasco. Must go, I have to finish building a built-in bookcase for a customer and then make a lasagne for Mum and Dad.

Love from Cath xx

November 5

DEAR FE,

It was such a relief to know that you are all right. I have been worried sick about you. If you're going away again, can you please let me know? Anyway, I liked your postcard of the emperor's palace in Kyoto, especially all the autumn colours.

This is a short reply as I'm nearly asleep on my feet. Our business is suddenly booming. Of course, it could just be the pre-Christmas rush, but we're actually thinking of putting on more staff in the New Year if this keeps up.

I do wish Jane would hurry up and get better. We could offer her a job. She'd be great at some of the gardening projects. As you know she's always been a keen gardener and has done a horticulture course.

However, I agree we should proceed with caution and not expand too fast. Or maybe I'm too cautious. Gaye and Pam have big ideas – when Bob comes back, Pam thinks we should ask him to do a feasibility study about us setting up a franchise. I still think she's being overly ambitious because really we've only just started, but Pam says you have to have a vision.

It's after midnight. I hope this finds you in good spirits and well rested after your holiday. It was nice of David to keep in touch. Grandma and Grandpa are fine.

Love from Mum xx

November 6

Dear Amy

Of course Fe is alive and well. I heard from her yesterday and she has been having a wonderful time travelling with some girlfriends. They went to Kyoto on the bullet train and did some sightseeing. Now she's back she is hard at work at Tailfeathers again and taking Japanese lessons.

I'm glad the girls liked their earrings and Dakota liked his jigsaw and Sydney liked his blocks. I'm looking forward to seeing you all again.

We are all working ten hours plus per day, but I am loving it. I get to meet some interesting people.

Love from Mother x

November 9

Dear Virginia and Georgia

I am sorry you thought the earrings looked 'daggy' and that Dakota and Sydney didn't like their presents either. That's life, I'm afraid. You can't always get what you want.

Love from Grandma xx

November 10

ATTENTION: LUCY FINDLAY (PRIVATE AND CONFIDENTIAL)

Yes, Bob's back from London. I was so glad to see him. I didn't realise how much I depended on him being around. He brought me some French perfume, and also a digital camera so I can take photos of our projects and send them to you and Fe and Amy. And he bought a box of Swiss chocolates for Mum and Dad. Isn't he thoughtful? I feel quite spoilt.

Speaking of spoilt, I never thought I'd hear myself saying this but I think my grandchildren are becoming spoilt little brats. The earrings I sent the girls weren't expensive enough – they've been brand-indoctrinated. Dakota is fast heading the same way and flushed his jigsaw puzzle down the loo because he wanted a Bazooka Blaster. At least Sydney's young enough to appreciate his blocks. (Though Amy's now enrolled him in Patterned Toddling, so who knows?)

Our children wouldn't have dared behave like that, would they? I'm sure it doesn't help that Dwayne's so busy at work. He's been applying for other jobs – I hope he gets one. How Amy manages to chauffeur them around all over the place I don't know, seeing as she is working at the suicide place, but she says that if she works from seven to three and has no lunch break she can finish early.

It's strange how things change. Amy was the very organised, independent big sister and Fe was always the dependent baby of the family, quite wilful and impetuous. But now Fe seems to be growing more independent, doing all that travelling virtually on her own. In fact, I think Fe's really grown up while she's been away and I think it's been good for her, even though I had my doubts and have worried about her constantly.

Amy, on the other hand, has become quite needy. She desperately wants me to come and stay. I think she's really tired. Working full-time and always trying to keep up with the Joneses must be a strain.

She seemed to handle her father's death in her usual cool, calm way, but I sometimes wonder if all this frantic activity is her way of trying to avoid dealing with it. Of course, she'd left home long before he died, so maybe she wasn't as close to him as Fe in the end. I really should broach the subject, but as you know we haven't been able to talk closely about much at all since she went to Sydney and met Dwayne. We've been trying lately, but her values seem to have changed so much. Should I talk to her or let things be, do you think?

If you ask me, Dwayne has it easy. He just goes to work, comes home, drives the kids to activities at weekends, and has a lot of what he calls 'down time' with his golfing mates. He doesn't do any repairs around the house, or gardening. They have a cleaner and a gardener, and the cars get *taken* to the car wash. They eat a lot of takeaway or they dine out, or dinner is pasta and salad. Never a roast. I don't think those kids would even know what a roast is.

Anyway, enough about all that. It does sound a good idea to rent out your apartment and move into Colin's house in Brighton after you're married. Meanwhile, we'd better make a date for getting the dresses fitted, hadn't we? And do you want me to give you a bridal shower?

I haven't heard from Jane for a while. Did you know they've put a computer in her room, so she can record her thoughts as some sort of therapy?

Must do a load of washing. It's eleven p.m. and I haven't changed the sheets for a fortnight.

Pam thinks we could branch out eventually, buy old houses, do them up and sell them. We could start with one and work on it at weekends, she says. I'd like to do that, and help stop all the demolition (and perhaps make some money). Bob says it's a good idea, but that we'd have to think about capital-gains tax.

Personally I think we should stick to what we're doing for at least twelve months. The track record for small businesses in this country isn't great. Lots of them fail because they expand too quickly, or because they're crippled by overheads and taxes. I heard that on talkback. How anyone actually gets rich legally in this country is beyond me, what with all the taxes and GST.

Anyway, in the distant future we might just buy an old house with our pooled money. At least, being single, we don't have to defer to any men about our decisions. Only our financial advisers and bank managers! But it's too early in the piece to worry about all this. We need to cope with what we're doing and not grow too quickly. Well, that's my opinion.

Got to stop, my eyes can hardly focus.

Love from Cath xx

November 10

DEAR AMY,

You had absolutely no right to read my PRIVATE AND CONFIDENTIAL email to Lucy. It was sent in error – apparently there's a computer virus that picks names randomly from your address book and sends them your emails. You should've realised immediately that it was not for your eyes.

I am sorry that you had to learn a few home truths from me in such a way, but then I'd never have been game to tell you face to face.

It's true that I don't think the children should be so scheduled and I think you work too hard and Dwayne should pull his weight more around the house. And I don't like hearing that he thinks I am wasting 'your inheritance' and half-killing myself with manual work at my age. This is my life, not yours. I love you all very much, but I don't like the way the children are becoming so materialistic.

It's late, I'm tired from sanding back doors.

Love from your mother xx

November 12

DEAR VIRGINIA AND GEORGIA,

No, I am not making money selling houses. Yes, I am sorry that you and your parents are mad at me, but sometimes relationships can only grow if we clear the air.

I love you all – never forget that.

I only want the best for you. That doesn't mean the best clothes and best toys, it means I want you to have the best happy lives from doing simple things, like going for a walk or baking cakes or growing your own vegies or playing board games with your friends. And most importantly, you need time for daydreaming and using your imaginations. I wish you didn't live so far away, then and we could do lots of these things at weekends and after school.

Love from Grandma. xxxx

November 13

Dear Amy,

I am glad the girls showed you my email. I am sorry that it made you cry. I know that you and Dwayne are trying to do your best for the children, it's just that my idea of 'best' and yours are poles apart. But if what I said has made you both stop and think about what you enjoyed most in your own childhoods, the simple things like going camping in pup tents and hiking and making daisy chains, then I'm glad I said it.

I think it is the first big disagreement we've ever had and I was very upset and churned up in the tummy. Now I hope we can forget it and move on (I've caught that expression from Lucy). And maybe you and I need to sit down and talk about your father's death, because we never have. Since Fe has been away, she and I have talked more openly about our feelings via email. Probably I wasn't ready to talk about your father's death before, but I am now and if you would like to I will take time off and fly up to Sydney next weekend and we can have a good talk and a good cry together.

Lots of love from your mum xxx

November 14

DEAR FE,

Yes, just about everyone read my email to Lucy – including Amy, Dwayne, the girls, Jane, you, all the weirdos who have ever emailed me, my bank manager, Bob's secretary, Simply Handywomen . . . One of life's little ironies. It's certainly taught me to be more careful. I've installed a new anti-virus program, so it shouldn't happen again.

Anyway, Amy and I have sorted out our differences now and I have suggested that I fly to Sydney for a mother–daughter chat about how we feel – a bit like you and I have been doing in our emails.

Thank you for sending the children a parcel, even if everything came from the 100-yen shop (that must be like a $2 shop?). Amy said the girls loved the hair clips and jewellery and bibs and bobs. Though I must say I'm not sure about mobile-phone accessories and make-up at their age. Anyway, the sumo doll was perfect for Dakota, Amy said, and Sydney loves his origami mobile too. It just goes to show yet again that the girls don't have to have expensive trinkets. Thanks also for my parcel. The little massage octopus works a treat on my shoulders and I love the scarf and the colourful pantyhose.

Pam and Gaye have been watching *Extreme Home Make-Overs* on TV and apparently if you can give a run-down house 'buyer appeal' with a fresh coat of paint and a nice garden you're sure to make a good profit when you sell. Personally I still think it's too soon for us to tackle anything that big. When would we get the time to do the renovations? Who would be running Simply Handywomen? It's not that I have no ambition, it's just that I'm more practical when it comes to how we would actually do it.

Don't get me wrong, I love Pam and Gaye. Thanks to them and Bob, I now have my own place finished, and the water feature and deck have definitely got 'buyer appeal'. (Not that I want to sell it.) The garden is looking very pretty with all the ranunculas and irises in bloom.

And I am very happy with the way Simple Handywomen is working out, even if it is time-consuming – it's not just a business, it's women achieving things together.

One minute I'm helping Pam fit shelves or Gaye is painting the corners, and the next we're all painting the walls and ceilings.

Of course we have our tense moments. The other day Pam yelled at me to stop, as she put it, 'standing round yacking as if you're at a garden party'. But we do operate so well as a team on the whole. I've had to give up SPUDS and Prime Movers and weight-resistance classes as there's just no time, but I'm getting fitter with all the physical work anyway. I'm shedding weight because I'm on the go all the time and not sitting around yacking and snacking on cakes and cuppas with Grandma like I was when she was living with me.

I still miss your father very much, though, despite my new and exciting life. Sometimes I feel sad that he's not here to see the bulbs in flower that he helped plant, but because I'm so busy I don't have time to brood. I think he'd be proud of me now, what with the house and starting Simply Handywomen. Though, of course, he was of the old school. He felt it was his job to earn the money and mine to stay home. Yes, on second thoughts I'm not so sure he'd approve of Simply Handywomen after all.

Grandpa had a small setback the other day. He climbed out his bedroom window and scaled the roof so he could shin down next-door's old apple tree, but the branch broke. He said he just wanted to go and buy some cigarettes – but he hasn't smoked for fifteen years. It just shows how the mind can revert to the past, doesn't it? He's okay, just a bit shaken and bruised. I've put some new locks on his window so that fresh air can come in but he can't climb out.

Gaye met a charming man when she was fixing his sister's toilet washer, and they're going out to dinner.

Hope everything is going well for you in Tokyo and you're saving lots of yen. You don't seem to have much time for casual boyfriends nowadays, which is good.

Love from Mum xxx

November 14

Attention: Lucy Findlay (Private and Confidential)

Thanks for your phone call. I'm glad you finally got my email. Yes, Amy was furious, but we talked it out and we achieved 'a certain amount of closure and she was able to move on', as you would say. The children are moving on, too. Fewer scheduled activities and more at home, even like cooking.

And as for me, I'm moving on so fast my feet are

hardly touching the floor. All my clothes are starting to hang off me like rag bags, I'm losing so much weight. And I've toned up thanks to all the exercise with Simply Handywomen. By the time I stagger in the door at the end of the day I just have a quick meal and fall into bed.

It's exciting that Colin can join you in Sydney for the weekend. Will you take some time off work to sort out the wedding? I know you've said no more than twenty people, but it still takes organising.

I haven't heard from Jane. *She* got my email too, because of the computer the hospital organised for her. Of course Julie read it, and she replied on Jane's behalf. I've cut and pasted it, so you can see for yourself!

Dear Cath,

I opened your email despite noting the PRIVATE AND CONFIDENTIAL, because I realised that you wanted me to read it. There is no such thing as an accidental email: you know I supervise Jane and your subconscious reached out.

I do not dispense free advice by email, but I will say that you appear to have a number of psychological problems, especially about how you perceive yourself as a woman in today's society.

> Your old-fashioned values and your refusal to accept that young children may be psychologically damaged if they are overly controlled and repressed by adults, suggest you would benefit from some attitudinal conformity therapy.
>
> Sincerely, Julie Danbratheberger

Isn't that the biggest load of rubbish? I was going to reply but couldn't even be bothered typing 'PIss off, dip shit!' (I learnt that phrase from Pam). I'm fine, thanks very much, and it's none of her business how I relate to my grandchildren, unless of course I was mistreating them in any way.

With Julie around, there's not much likelihood of Jane returning to her old self for the time being. I know you wanted her to be your bridesmaid too, but there's no chance of it, really. You saw what she was like. Short of kidnapping her, I don't know what we can do. I suppose she has to go through all this if she's to get well.

I'm getting stirred up again and that won't solve the problem, will it? When you're back from Sydney, let's have lunch. I can come up to Melbourne and meet you at Southbank.

Love as always, Cath xx

November 15

ATTENTION: LUCY FINDLAY (PRIVATE AND CONFIDENTIAL)

Remember how we used to speak pig Latin? Then read this. Do not mention idnappingkay anejay. Internet security could get upset when the word idnapkay is mentioned.

Love from Cath xx

November 15

You can't remember pig latin? I said not to mention kidnapping Jane because Big Brother Internet security is watching and red flags will pop up.

Love as always, Cath

November 16

DEAR FE,

I'm so happy you'll be home for Lucy's wedding. I am going to be the only bridesmaid now: Jane was too, but she really can't. Unless there is a miracle – I'm very worried about her.

Anyway, moving along. I can't believe how many yen you've saved. Bob suggests you convert them into Aussie dollars through a bank before you leave Japan, and you'll need at least a week to do it.

Bob and I went out with Gaye and Pam and Allen and Tom and we had a really good dinner. I think I told you that Gaye met a nice man when she was doing a toilet cistern? Well, that's Allen. And Bob introduced his solicitor friend Tom to Pam and they've started going out together. Pam is still a bit edgy – I think she thinks Tom's too good to be true. She said to me, 'If I dig too deeply I'll probably find out he's got major flaws,' so she's remaining a bit distant.

Of course, she's been very hurt by men in the past. I told Bob this and he's probably told Tom, because he's being an absolute gentleman. We may all go out again next week. It's actually nice to have a gentleman escort without any of the innuendoes and harassment. But I don't have much time for socialising, as business is booming.

The Ginza sounds fascinating, with all those unusual shops. But you going on a harbour cruise in the moonlight made me uneasy, even if they were 'wealthy businessmen'. Were your friends with you? Always be careful – those men may have been very nice, but some mightn't be.

It's late, midnight, and I have to get some sleep. Do keep in touch.

Love from Mum xx

November 18

LUCY FINDLAY (PRIVATE AND CONFIDENTIAL)

You'll never guess who just knocked on my door. Jane! She left the hospital and got a taxi here. She said it was all right being in hospital when she was in a really bad way, but once her head started getting clearer she just wanted to go home. Julie kept saying she wasn't ready, so she simply walked out.

Anyway, I put her to bed in the spare room and I've just phoned Bob. It's the middle of the night but he was terrific – he told me to keep her here and he'd phone the hospital to let them know she's safe. He's going to ring Tom first thing in the morning to get any legalities sorted out, if there are any. He also suggested that Jane see another doctor, just to make sure that she'd be all right living at home. I agree that's a good idea.

Just wanted to let you know. It's now three a.m. and I am so tired I can hardly keep my eyes open. I'll write again soon and let you now what happens. But the good news is that Jane seems to be okay now.

Love Cath xx

November 19

DEAR AMY

I can't believe your wonderful news! Please give Dwayne my congratulations and a hug – heading up a new division, *and* with a substantial increase in salary. But best of all from my point of view is that the job's in Melbourne!

It's all a bit much for me to take in at the moment. So sudden. But so exciting.

If Dwayne will be earning more, you might even be able to be a stay-at-home mum? We'll be able to get together for lunch and I can be more of a 'hands-on' grannie. As you know, I'm very busy with Simply Handywomen, but I'll make time, especially at weekends, to do things with the children. We'll be able to have such adventures. There's the zoo and the beaches and Scienceworks and all sorts of fun. Adventure Grannie, here I come.

Lots of love from Mum xxxxx

November 20

ATTENTION: LUCY FINDLAY (PRIVATE AND CONFIDENTIAL)

Just to update you further re Jane. Tom told her the hospital can't force her to stay there. She's still a bit vague, because it takes a while for the drugs to leave your system, but she's much more like her old self. I'm sure she'll be okay.

She's keen to go back to her own place rather than stay here. Because Derek left 'the conjugal home' to live with Marcus, and hasn't been looking after it, she can legally move back in straight away. After the property settlement, either she can buy out his share or the house can be sold.

She says Derek doesn't want anything to do with Bryan at the moment, so as Bryan needs a stable home while he gets himself sorted out, he'll live with Jane. But she's determined that he get a job and pay board and stop bleeding her dry. Do you know, I actually think her breakdown was good for her – it's helped her get her priorities straight and has somehow made her stronger.

She's keen to do some part-time work, so she can come and be the Simply Handywomen gardener after all. I can't believe everything is working out so well.

Sadly, one thing that didn't work out so well is Gaye and Allen. They broke up. He used to be a school-teacher and he kept saying in her ear during sex, 'Is it good, is it good?' and then afterwards, 'Was it good?' Then he wanted her to give him a mark out of ten. Gaye said, 'How could I say he was actually a bit of a dud and I'd only give him five?'

An estate agent came around offering free valuations and he said he could sell this house for nearly triple what we paid for it. But I love it and I don't want to sell. I can't wait for Fe to see it. I've made so many little improvements while she's been away.

Speaking of Fe, she's delighted you're asking her to the wedding. And Amy is very excited that you want Virginia and Georgie as junior bridesmaids and Dakota as the pageboy. Of course, Sydney's still too young. Anyway, they're planning to come to Melbourne just before Christmas and look for a place to rent until they find what Amy calls 'the right home'.

I agree that Tibby should give you away if Rohan can't come, but I'm sure he'll fly over. It's not every day that your mother gets married on a tropical island. It would be nice if both your children could give you away.

I'm not surprised the guest list has blown out to sixty. There's Colin's relatives and friends as well as yours. But will everyone be able to fly to Daydream Island? Maybe they won't all attend.

It was lovely of you to invite Robert and Helene. Of course you've known them for years, but . . . And my parents, though I don't expect they'd be able to manage the flight. Well, Dad might, and Bob could help look after him while I'm bridesmaiding, but Mum couldn't. Never mind, they can watch the video.

Bouquets of baby pineapples and berries entwined with tropical vines is certainly an unusual idea. But orchids would be a bit ordinary, I agree. And a conch-shell fanfare – it's great that Colin is happy to cater to your every whim.

And he's bought you some sapphire and diamond earrings? How lucky can you be to find a man with money who's genuinely kind, intelligent and sexy. They're thin on the ground, as I well know.

Love from Cath xx

November 23

Dear Fe,

I was HORRIFIED to learn that you have taken a job on Sundays at a place called The Strip House! There must be other ways to earn 'heaps of money' than by working in a strip club, surely. I will be very glad when you are back home again, safe and sound.

I've had a talk to Bob about your finances and he thinks you should send some money to your Australian account now, because things will shut down over Christmas and he can get you a good interest rate.

You asked about Jane. She is so much better, and she's really happy doing some gardening part-time with Pam, and although we are flat-chat we're all getting along like a house on fire. Speaking of which, Mrs Jabobi's house – you know it, two down from Peg's – caught on fire. A faulty wire in the ceiling. Luckily it was just the two front rooms, but she wants us to do the repair work once the insurance is sorted out (not the rewiring and major work, just painting and small repairs). We're getting a lot of work by word of mouth.

Now, Lucy's wedding. Amy says the girls are so looking forward to being bridesmaids. As a surprise they're busy choreographing a little ballet to the music of *Swan Lake*, only as it's Daydream Island they'll probably be dying seagulls, not swans. And now that Virginia is learning the cello and Georgia the saxophone, they're also planning a surprise musical recital. They are talented children, to say the least. I wonder if Dwayne can use some of his frequent flyer points to buy a seat for the cello?

I know Amy told you about moving to Melbourne. Who knows, Dwayne might even be able to arrange a job for you if you ask him.

Remember to look after yourself properly, won't you?

Love from Mum xx

P.S. Who is Jungi? Is he the one with his hand round your waist in the photo of you standing with the Tokyo Tower sort of sprouting out of your head?

November 25

Dear Fe

Oh, sorry, you meant The Stripe House and it's an art gallery. See how useful a spell-checker is? You should use it!

Must go, so much happening here.

Love from Mum xx

November 26

Dear Jane

It seems funny emailing you when I only saw you last night. Your Handywomen colleagues really enjoyed that lovely supper, thanks.

Yes, let's get together for Gaye's birthday and have dinner out somewhere. We can all put in for a present.

Just enjoy each day at a time, dear friend, and try not to do too much all at once, okay? We want you well and happy for Lucy's wedding.

Love, Cath

November 29

ATTENTION: LUCY FINDLAY (PRIVATE AND CONFIDENTIAL)

Come on, Lucy, do you really think Jane would appreciate a bloke leaping out of a cake for Gaye's birthday? Some things never change: Jane might have had a breakdown, but she hasn't had a personality implant! So it's Edwardo's for a nice elegant dinner, with drinks at Marnie's Bar beforehand.

We've clubbed together and bought Gaye a new set of tools (which we can claim on tax) and some perfume and chocolates, (which we can't). Your share is $30. I'll get you to sign the card before we all meet. That is, if you get to Marnie's in time. Otherwise you'll have to sign it in front of her.

Bryan has managed to get a legitimate job with a computer firm. Apparently he thinks that subconsciously he knew his father was queer and he turned to drugs to cope. Sounds like an excuse to me. I mean, Derek was always the same, wasn't he? He didn't act gay, he took Bryan fishing and racing at the Speedway and dirt-bike riding and hiking and all those father–son things. He seemed normal to me. That doesn't sound right, if you're gay you're normal except you're gay, if you get what I mean.

Gaye says drug addicts do that – always blame someone else, never themselves, because it's easier.

So the guest list is now at a hundred and thirty-one! Never mind, you only get married once. Or twice, in your case. Or three times, in Colin's case. But this will be IT for you both, so you might as well have a big crowd and hang the expense.

Don't get stressed by those snobby Brighton matrons, you're as good if not better than them. I know they're probably chagrined (how do you like that word, I got it from the thesaurus because I wanted a word that was more ladylike than 'pissed off') that you've nabbed him.

Anyway, I have to go but I'll just tell you about dinner with Bob last night. It was at the new seafood restaurant by the bay (Bob's the silent partner in it). They've got an excellent chef, a young chap who's come from some restaurant up north. For starters I had a prawn and avocado medley and Bob had deep-fried prawns with lime butter. Then I had barramundi and Bob had a whole baby schnapper. Lovely crisp salad. Very nice. Bob didn't fancy dessert, but of course I did. White chocolate cheese cake with a dark chocolate base. So much for the weight loss!

Tomorrow it's back to work as usual. Hope everything is okay with you – do you want me to get anything organised at this end? I must say it's marvellous that everything's being done by Daydream. Much less stress all round. I just remembered how when you and Barry got married you were pregnant with Rohan and wearing all that white tulle.

Must go.

Love as always, Cath xx

December 1

DEAR MICHIKO

I am very grateful for you letting me know that Fe is in hospital. How did she fall down the stairs? I will phone the hospital immediately and make arrangements to fly to Tokyo. Thank you for being such a caring mama-san.

Sincerely, Catherine Morgan

December 1

DEAR AMY

I tried phoning you several times but your answer machine seems to be on the blink. This is URGENT. Fe is in hospital in Tokyo with concussion and a sprained ankle. I'm making arrangements to fly there as soon as I can. Bob is organising the tickets. I'm in a hurry.

Love from your mother xx

December 2

ATTENTION: LUCY FINDLAY (PRIVATE AND CONFIDENTIAL)

I am in the Qantas lounge using their computer.

I still can't believe it. I breastfed that girl for eleven months, I made sure she got her inoculations, drank her Milo and ate silverbeet and red meat and eggs and lots of fruit. I made her wear a seatbelt. And since she's been overseas I've sent her crates of Eternal Life vitamins and singlets and stuff to keep her healthy. And what does she do? Trip down some bloody stairs. Unbelievable. But I must calm down or I'll have palpitations.

I hope I can cope with everything over there – it's my first trip away alone. Luckily, Bob has contacted an old friend who is an academic and a member of the International House of Japan, so I'm staying there. It's in Roppongi and apparently only one train stop from Hiroo and the hospital. Thank heavens I made Fe take out medical insurance before she left.

Fortunately I already had a passport – remember, I got one when Fe first went away, just in case I had to fly over and rescue her. Bob organised an emergency visa for me, and here I am.

Bob really has been marvellous. He even offered to take time off and go with me. He's a man in a million. I said I'd be okay, because I know he's so busy just before

Christmas with the new restaurant and all the other things he's involved in.

Anyway, I'll email you when I get to Roppongi. Bob's friend is going to meet me at the airport and take me to the hospital.

Love, Cath xx

December 3

Dear Amy

I know it was bad timing for you, what with Dwayne in Germany and Dakota with chickenpox, but don't worry. There's no need for you to fly out, as Fe isn't as bad as they thought. She hasn't got concussion, just a lump on her head as big as a chook's egg and the sprained ankle.

The hospital is squeaky-clean and Fe has a private room all to herself, thanks to having top health cover. She's in good spirits and eager to come home.

I'm writing this at International House. They've been very helpful. I have a quiet room on the second floor, with a shower and toilet and twin beds. There's a sliding door that opens onto a balcony overlooking the most beautiful Japanese-style garden with ancient little lanterns and pagodas and a pool with what look like huge goldfish but which I'm told are Japanese carp. The room is 15 000 yen per night (that's about $220 Australian) and includes a cooked breakfast. Apparently this rate is extremely reasonable for the middle of Tokyo.

I can't make coffee or tea in my room, but just down the hall is a machine that dispenses hot and cold drinks in cans for around 400 yen. Isn't that amazing, canned hot coffee, and I can get black, milk, cappuccino or latte.

I went to see Mama-san at Tailfeathers, which is not far from International House – in fact, straight down my street for a couple of blocks, then just around a corner. She was really nice. The club seemed quite neat and tidy really, apart from smelling of stale alcohol – you know, that sort of pub smell. She showed me the place where Fe tripped and I could see that it must have been Fe's fault as the carpet was quite new-looking, no torn bits or ragged edges she could have caught her heel in. Mama-san apologised and said she couldn't keep Fe's place open but that she had been very popular with the customers and could come back any time. She gave me the money owed to Fe, and bowed politely. Her English was very good.

Japanese people are very polite. And very clean. Even the taxis are spotless. They have snow-white cloths with a lace edging on the front and back seats, and the rear passenger side door opens and closes automatically. The drivers get quite annoyed if you shut the door manually because it messes up their system or something. Also I went to see the people at The Stripe House (not the Strip House – I got that wrong). It's an art gallery at Imo-arai-taka (that means 'hill') where Fe was working on Sundays to earn extra money, giving out programs and speaking to English tourists.

The doctors say that Fe will be able to fly home in a couple of days. I'm making arrangements – luckily she has an open ticket. Hopefully we'll be able to get a flight on Friday.

Meanwhile, I'll try and see a bit of Tokyo in between hospital visits.

Love from your mother xx

P.S. I'm sorry Sydney's teething again. Do wish the girls luck for their ballet final.

December 3

DEAR VIRGINIA AND GEORGIA,

Your Aunty Fe is okay and you'll see her at Christmas time. She can't buy you any gifts because she's in hospital, but I'll go to the 100 yen shop and see what I can find.

Love from Grandma

(and big xx for Dakota and Sydney too)

December 3

DEAR JANE, GAYE, AND PAM AKA SIMPLY HANDYWOMEN

I'm eternally grateful to all of you for popping in to see if Mum and Dad are okay. I phoned them yesterday and Mum said you'd brought around some lovely cakes and magazines. And thanks for feeding Harriet and Henry too, and watering the garden.

All is fine here. I saw the mama-san from Tailfeathers and she was very polite, but I wouldn't like to cross her. I think she'd be the iron fist in the velvet glove. She was very careful to show me the stairs where Fe tripped and I could see that it was brand-new carpet. However, I had no intention of suing them, so she needn't have worried.

Now I have to arrange to retrieve Fe's things from her apartment. I'll also have to find out if she needs to pay her share of rent until they can find another girl to take her place.

I hope SH is going well.

I'll be home as soon as I can.

Love from Cath xx

December 4

DEAR BOB

You are a saint. Thank you for your call and thank you from the bottom of my heart for organising for us to fly home first-class. As you pointed out, Fe will be able to put her seat right back and rest her ankle. Such luxury for us both.

I'm profoundly grateful and looking forward to seeing you very soon.

Cheers, Cath

December 4

ATTENTION: LUCY FINDLAY (PRIVATE AND CONFIDENTIAL)

I was so relieved to see Fe sitting up bright as a button in her hospital bed flirting with the young Japanese doctor that I didn't have the heart to be cross with her. I suppose anyone can fall down some stairs, though I suspect she was drunk. But if she was she certainly wouldn't tell me.

International House is very clean with friendly staff and surrounded by a beautiful Japanese garden. I'm grateful Bob's friend Theodore is a member here, which is why I was allowed to stay. It's actually a conference and study centre for cultural/educational exchange worldwide, so there are mainly academics staying here, although I chatted to one American woman over breakfast who's here studying the Japanese harp. According to her it's a very difficult instrument to play.

It's much nicer than staying in a hotel because it's more homely and I can leave the door to the balcony open to let in the fresh air (I'm on the second floor), even though the weather is chilly.

It's apparently very safe in Japan. It's part of their culture to be honest, and to be kind to children and old people. They say you can walk the streets at night and not be molested. Although this place is slap-bang in the middle of Tokyo, it's extremely quiet.

Fe is allowed to fly home on Friday, so I'll do a little sightseeing in between sorting out her belongings and hospital visits. I might even go to a mixed public bath. Anyway, I'd better get ready to go to the hospital. I'll get them to call me a cab, but tomorrow I'll try catching the train. It's only one station away. How hard can that be?

Just as well Fe isn't part of the wedding party. But at least she'll be able to come, even if she's still on crutches.

Love from Cath and love to Colin xxx

December 5

DEAR BOB

Thanks for your email. I'm not surprised you couldn't get through on the phone this time – the phones here seem to be constantly in use. Sorry I sent such a brief email yesterday – I was in a bit of a tizz.

I'm just off to visit Fe. Sayonara (that means goodbye) and see you on Saturday. The plane leaves at eight-fifteen and it's Flight QF 180, but you already know that, of course, because you booked our seats.

It's a funny thing, but I have to confess that I miss your twinkly eyes, and again huge thanks from both of us. Take care of yourself. See you soon.

Cheers, Cath

December 5

ATTENTION: LUCY FINDLAY (PRIVATE AND CONFIDENTIAL)

Heavens, what a bolt from the blue! You were talking to Colin about Rohan and Tibby when they were little and he said he'd like a child because he can afford to give one a very good life? Lucy, you haven't got a womb. Have you told him that small fact? And, bloody hell, you're fifty-five!

I really don't think you should go into marriage with

this hanging over your head. You need to sort it out. Children take up a lot of time, as you well know, and are a big commitment. But I don't want to interfere. It's your lives.

Fe has a constant host of visitors round her bed. She seems to know everyone in Tokyo. I feel quite superfluous, even though she says she loves me being there.

Yesterday I did go to the hospital by the subway train. The signs are in Japanese and English, but even in English they don't have straight-out place names like Ferntree Gully. Try and get your tongue around Kasumigaseki and Akabane-bashi, or Ga-ku-gai-Dai-ga-ku.

Anyway, I paid the 160 yen for a ticket to Hiroo, but somehow I got on an express train that I didn't know was an express. When it finally stopped, I figured that if I got a train going the other way it would take me back to Roppongi. That's what it said on the station map. However, somehow I read the arrows wrongly and ended up on an express to Yokohama forty minutes away from Tokyo.

Then I couldn't get through the turnstile because I'd only paid 160 yen, but a kind lady showed me a fare-adjustment machine. By then I decided I might as well have a look round Yokahama, which is quite pleasant. I tried to phone Fe with my mobile, but of course it wouldn't work. And there was no way I could cope with a public phone in Japanese, so I had a cup of coffee at the station and then bought another ticket to Hiroo.

I was surprised to see all these little school-children on their own, walking round the streets and on the train. I've been wondering why our society seems to be so violent and theirs isn't. I suspect it's because they are taught respect and their way of life is very structured and traditional. It's part of the culture for men to have female company other than their wives, like in the hostess bars or the 'love hotels'. So while they're doing that they're not running around raping people. Well, that's my theory.

Fe told me I'm not supposed to blow my nose or eat in public (except for an ice-cream, which is acceptable if one has to), which is why the streets aren't littered with empty wrappers and packets and cans. I'm enjoying the food. The yakitori and noodle bars are good and not expensive. They have plastic samples of the food in the windows and you just drag the waiter outside and point to what you want.

I was only joking about the mixed public baths. I have found a bath near the hospital, with separate areas for men and women, and I'm going today after I've collected Fe's things from her apartment, which I imagine will be a messy job.

Yes, we'll get our final fittings next week. And yes,

Amy matched the swatch of material perfectly for the girls' dresses, didn't she? But have you thought that high heels in sand might be difficult?

Love as always from Cath xx

December 6

Oh, sorry. Colin meant adopting a refugee child. Sometimes I don't read things properly. But frankly, I think you're too old. Wouldn't it be better to sponsor one through World Vision or something?

Your confused friend Cath xx

December 7

DEAR VIRGINIA AND GEORGIA

Yes, Grandma is coming home tomorrow with Aunty Fe. Yes, I heard you've been fitted for your bridesmaid dresses in Sydney. And Dakota for his outfit. And yes, I bought you some nice things from the 100 yen shop.

No, I have not eaten raw squid. The food is lovely, lots of noodles and rice.

Love from Grandma xx

December 7

DEAR HANDYWOMEN

Hopefully I'll be back at work on Monday. I hope it's not too hot, because the change in climate and working in that attic job will probably knock me for six. Jetlag shouldn't be a problem, because there's only a two-hour time difference and Fe and I can lie back and sleep all night on the plane.

Bob is meeting us at the airport and driving us home, so you don't need to worry about that. See you on Monday unless you have time to drop around over the weekend. Can you please let my mum and dad know that we'll be home safe and sound very soon.

Love from Cath xx

December 9

ATTENTION: LUCY FINDLAY (PRIVATE AND CONFIDENTIAL)

We're back home safe and sound, though Fe is lying on the sofa with her ankle propped up on a cushion, complaining that everything's aching.

When we got to the airport, David, the chap she met in Egypt, was waiting for her. It turns out she's been corresponding with him since he came back to Australia.

Anyway, he seems very nice. He gave her one of those helium-filled balloons with 'Keep your spirits up!' written on it. He's coming to take her out on the weekend.

Of course, as planned, Bob was waiting for us too. He was holding a red rose for me and a yellow one for Fe. He said he'd missed me, pulled me into his arms and kissed me full on the lips in front of Fe and everybody. And it was really strange – I tingled right down from my head to my toes. It definitely wasn't jetlag. I immediately pulled back, because . . . well, I'm not sure why. Probably shock. So now I'm not sure how to act around him. I feel like a teenager who's got a crush and doesn't know what to do about it.

I really enjoyed Japan and would love to go back there to explore everything at leisure one day. I only saw parts of Tokyo, though I did manage to get a good view from the Tokyo Tower (I walked there, which took about fifteen minutes). I also took a short bus tour which went to the Imperial Palace. Just a short stop at the outer garden, we didn't actually go in and have green tea with the emperor or anything. Then we went to the Asakusa Buddhist temple, which was fascinating.

Must go. I'll see you Tuesday for our final fittings. Then onto the bridal shower!

Love as always, Cath

December 11

ATTENTION: LUCY FINDLAY (PRIVATE AND CONFIDENTIAL)

It'll be strange not having to write Private and Confidential any more. When are you finishing up at work – tomorrow, or the day after?

Don't our dresses look gorgeous? And how lucky to find matching shoes, even though we'll probably get bogged in the sand.

I can't believe the presents you got at your bridal shower. I love that white Wedgwood teaset. And the beautiful oriental vase from Fe. I didn't know my daughter had such good taste. Speaking of Fe, did I tell you she's already got an interview for a job with Dwayne's company? They need new people straight away, and apparently he put in a word for her at the Melbourne office. The job isn't in his section, which is probably a good thing, and she'd be using her marketing degree at last. She's so excited. So fingers crossed, though I've said to her that if this one doesn't work out there'll be other jobs. I don't want her to get her hopes up and then have them dashed.

In a way, it will be good if Fe moves to Melbourne. Two determined females like us living in the same house isn't easy, as I'm finding out. She's more into contemporary furnishings, and though she loves what I've done with the house (and has been sunbaking on the new deck), she likes what she calls 'sharp clean lines' and lots of glass and chrome (heavens, sounds like Helene). She says she'd love to live in one of those new warehouse apartments near Docklands. But of course that would cost a fortune. I guess it all depends on whether this new job pans out and how much it pays.

No, I haven't told Bob how I felt when he kissed me. And don't you dare breathe a word, either! I value his friendship so much, and if he thought I was keen on him he'd run a mile in the opposite direction. I'm sure he just likes me as a good friend and the widow of his old mate, even if he did give me what seemed like a more-than-friendly kiss at the airport. Thinking back, he was probably just glad to see me.

So it's only a few days before we're on Daydream Island. I hope Cyclone Agnes stays well out to sea. We don't need gale-force winds for the ceremony.

Love as always, Cath

December 13

Omigod, Lucy, I heard it on the news. I thought that after the last cyclone they'd made everything cyclone-proof up north. So all travel and accommodation there is cancelled? You'll get your money back, I'm sure. We won't panic.

But WHAT ABOUT THE WEDDING?

Love from your frantic friend Cath xx

December 13

Right. Good suggestion from Colin. We'll have the wedding at his house and you'll still be getting married on sand by the water, just as planned. Now, leave everything to us Handywomen. You're not to worry about a thing.

Love as always, Cath xx

December 13

Lucy, I know the ambience won't be quite the same, what with cargo ships in the background and seaweed in the foreground, but by the time SH has finished decorating you won't notice a thing. Trust me! Just get Colin to meet us there at nine with the keys, okay, so we can get started.

Love as always, Cath xx

December 13

DEAR JANE,

Yes, Pam already has tables and chairs organised. Bob's friend Paul knows a chap who'll whip up a three-tiered cake at short notice. And a wedding celebrant. Bob knows another chap who'll provide the cars at a reasonable price. Gaye's organising people to bring in tropical plants and potted palms, and we're buying some of those bamboo flares for the garden and the beach. I'm arranging accommodation for the guests.

We need to get there early to set up the tables. I've hired white linen tablecloths, crockery, cutlery and glasses. Thank God for computers and websites and emails.

Love, Cath xx

December 14

DEAR FE

Thank God you can organise the flowers through Ali's sister. Fancy her having a florist shop. I know Lucy had her heart set on tropical arrangements, but Singapore orchids will be lovely. I'm so relieved your ankle's feeling a bit better and you can walk without the crutches.

Amy and Dwayne are now moving down before

Christmas. Dwayne was supposed to start the new job in January, but there's been some big hassle, someone's got shunted overseas and they want him to start earlier. It's all very sudden and very hectic. Bob has an estate-agent friend called George who's already found a house in Camberwell they could rent for three months while they look for a place to buy. Apparently it's got five bedrooms and a swimming pool, so I'm sure the children will like it. And it's furnished, so all they'd have to do is move in. Amy is hoping the girls won't be too upset with the move, what with having to start at a new school and getting all their other classes rescheduled. If they could buy a house in or near Camberwell, that would at least mean the girls won't have to change schools twice.

Brief Respite are helping out with Grandma and Grandpa so I can concentrate on the wedding. The forecast is for sunny weather. But you know how Melbourne can have four seasons in one day.

No, I truly don't mind you moving to Melbourne. Ali's flatmate moving out is too good an opportunity to miss, especially as the flat isn't far from Dwayne's company. I'm so thrilled you passed the first interview. Fingers crossed. And you explained your limp was only temporary? That's good.

So Ali's flat is modern and all glass and chrome, just like you wanted. No, don't feel guilty. Of course I'll miss you not being at home, but I've got my own life in order and have learnt to manage on my own. Though one day I might even feel ready to move on with a new partner, if that's what fate has in mind. As you said the other day, even you think it's time I looked for someone new, and I didn't think it at all disloyal to Dad. I *was* a bit surprised when you said 'Someone like Bob', after all the things you've said about him. Anyway, I'm glad you like him now.

Colin's such a kind man too. He knows that Lucy had her heart set on an island honeymoon, so now they're going to Tasmania. Which obviously isn't tropical, but it was all they could get at such short notice. And it is lovely.

Must go,

Love from Mum xx

December 14

DEAR AMY

Don't worry, George will meet you all at the airport and drive you straight to see the house in Camberwell.

It's lovely that you'll be in Melbourne for the school holidays and I'll be able to pop up when I'm not working.

Our work will probably slow down after Christmas and into the New Year while people are on holidays, so I'm anticipating we'll be able to do lots of things together with the children. I'm really looking forward to it.

Re the wedding. Yes, it's almost all under control. I know the girls are disappointed not to be going to a tropical island, but they can pretend that Brighton Beach is an island. Trying to get a caterer at such short notice was a nightmare but Gaye's cousin does catering with two friends, and by all accounts they do a lovely spread. She said she could cope if we had nibbles first and then a buffet. We're having large platters of seafood and cold collations, followed by tropical fruit. Colin has organised the drinks: beer, wines, soft drinks and champagne.

Having a buffet meal is good, especially as we didn't have time to organise place-cards. Lucy has decided that people can sit wherever they want to.

Did I tell you that the guest list blew out to a hundred and thirty and they're all coming? I think the only ones who aren't are your grandma and grandpa. As you can imagine, the whole thing's been a bit of a nightmare to re-organise, but I think we're there. Oh, Pam's friend Paula is a professional photographer. She's taking the photos and her partner will do a video.

I said to Pam and Gaye that we should expand ourselves to include Simply Weddings and they both jumped down my throat. Gaye said, 'Never again! If it was for anyone but Lucy they could go and get stuffed.'

Rohan and Tibby are both coming, which is fantastic. If you could take the children over to Colin's after Sydney's nap tomorrow, Lucy said they can have a rehearsal. We can press their frocks and Dakota's trousers at Colin's house.

Looking forward to seeing you all,

Love from your mother xx

December 15

Dear Fe,

I'm at Colin's house. The flowers have arrived and look gorgeous. Tell Ali thanks for organising them. We are very fortunate to have friends with connections. We always seem to fall on our feet and know someone to get us out of sticky situations.

Why I'm emailing you: I tried phoning but your battery must be flat. Can you come over at lunch-time and give us a hand? Things are even more frantic than anticipated. There's heaps of things you can do sitting down, like napkin-folding. And if Ali's free that'd be brilliant.

Rohan's plane got delayed and Tibby's jetlagged and no use whatsoever.

I am so glad that my children are energetic and useful.

Love from Mum xx

December 15

Dear Bob

Just wondering if you're still at the office. This is a big ask – can you possibly pick up Mum and Dad? They've changed their minds and want to come. Sorry about this, but there's no one else left: everyone is here. David would have driven down but he's at the airport waiting for Rohan's plane to come in. Can you phone Colin's house with a yes or no?

Cheers, Cath

December 15

Dear Bob

You are the dearest man. Yes, they can have a light meal before they come. As long as you're here by seven, that should be fine. We're having drinks and nibbles, then the ceremony's at sunset. And Colin has suggested that Mum and Dad might like to stay the night at his house. Can you make sure they have their medications and nightwear and spare underwear, please? Of course, if they're determined to go home I can drive them back after the wedding.

Cheers, Cath

December 15

Dear Bob

No confetti allowed, but Mum can throw rice because the seagulls will eat it later, so it won't be an environmental hazard.

Cheers Cath

December 18

Dear Fe

Wasn't it just wonderful? I'm exhausted, but I'm also on a high because the wedding was so beautiful. It was a great idea having the drinks by the pool. Not so good that Grandpa fell in fully dressed. Good that Colin had spare clothes that fitted.

I've already seen some of the video. We can all get copies. It starts before the wedding, with Pam up a ladder fixing the fairy lights and Gaye winding vine leaves through the trellis. And me rushing about with a teatowel making sure the glasses are clean. Close-ups of Jane setting the table, and you and David folding the napkins.

Then it cuts to Lucy in her apartment, and Jane and I arrive in a flurry and we all whizz off to the hairdresser. Then Amy and the girls arrive for their hair-dos. Back to Lucy's to get dressed. Scenes of us getting into the wedding cars. Then the actual wedding.

And wasn't it glorious? The sunset, with the sea bathed in those wonderful colours. I thought our dresses looked stunning against all the pink and orange clouds. Did you like Pam and Gaye's surprise sand island complete with moat and bridge, so Lucy got married on her 'island' after all, even if there was only room for her and Colin and the celebrant. I must say it was hard not to laugh when the waves from that motorboat washed over the island just as Lucy was saying 'I do'.

And the palm fronds and flares! It was all so pretty. Our heels kept getting bogged in the sand, but who cared? And weren't the girls lovely, doing their ballet against the dying sunset? I must say I was glad that Amy persuaded them not to do the musical recital as well, or we'd have been there till midnight. As it was, your grandma was very tired and getting fractious with Grandpa. I suppose it didn't help that he thought it was his wedding and that he was the one marrying Lucy, even if he did think it was Grandma. Old age is very confused and confusing some times.

Gaye's cousin's mob did a marvellous job with the catering. I had two helpings of that poached salmon with the lime and mango dressing. And wasn't the cake an absolute masterpiece? It must have been a metre high. I'm glad the photographer managed to photograph it before Dakota gouged out that huge chunk.

The only real drama was when your grandpa went missing. I think Grandma had got to the stage where she couldn't care less whether he came back or not. She had that pressed-lips thing happening. But when he was brought back and stood in the doorway with his face all lit up saying, 'Darling Lorna, I've been looking everywhere for you. Will you marry me?' she was struggling to hold back the tears. We all were, really.

Anyway, thanks for all your help, Fe. And a special thanks to Ali. Tell her from me she's an absolute gem.

Love from Mum xx

December 18

Dear Amy

Yes, it was a wonderful wedding, wasn't it? The girls looked gorgeous and Dakota was quite the little gentleman. I think he carried the cushion beautifully. It wasn't his fault he dropped the ring in the sand – Lucy was supposed to Velcro it on, but she thought I was doing it. Anyway, good old Bob dived on it before it disappeared.

And didn't everyone make a fuss of Sydney? He is such a happy baby. Just big, beaming smiles at everyone. It's a shame he's started biting, though. As the Day Care people said, it's just a passing phase, but a painful one.

The Camberwell house is lovely, isn't it? I was really impressed. Lots of room for the children, a study for Dwayne, and a lovely garden with beautiful old trees.

What are you going to do about your furniture in Sydney? I don't suppose there's any hurry, is there, until the house is sold. And with that amazing alarm system, your things will be safe.

It's all happening in such a hurry. It makes my head whirl.

Must go, love from your mother xx

December 19

DEAR LUCY

What on earth are you doing emailing me on your honeymoon. Of course I'm dying for a gossip about the wedding, but can't that wait till you get back?

No, we can't move Christmas lunch to Colin's, even though it *is* a beautiful house. It's definitely my turn this year, and now everyone's going to come here instead of Mum and Dad's. Fe and Amy, Dwayne and the children will all be together for the first Christmas since James died, so this is important to me. And Mum and Dad won't unravel if they only have to get to my place. The trip to Melbourne for the wedding was no good at all for Mum's spine. As for Dad, he was very confused by all the tropical ambience. The next day at Colin's he seemed to think he was David Niven in that movie on a desert island, and that Mum was Ava Gardner. It took all day to settle him down.

I want it just like we used to: the present-opening under the Christmas tree, and then lunch. But we could have high tea at Colin's later, if you like, so all the other Melbourne people can come. As well as Fe and Amy's lot. I don't think Robert and Helene will come – they always do their own thing at Christmas. Though if it's at Colin's house, they might.

Speaking of Helene, I must say that she did make an effort to spend time with Mum at the wedding. But wasn't her outfit dreadful. Black and silver for a beach wedding? And that hat. She looked like she was frocked up for the races at Flemington. I did think that Robert could have refrained from handing round his business cards. Bob spent quite a bit of time talking to Robert, which was nice of him.

It worked out well that Tibby and Rohan could stay on at Colin's and housesit. Rohan's grown into a nice young man. Remember how we used to hope he and Fe would get together? But I don't think they'd be a good match. He's too Londonised and she's too . . . Fe.

Yes, I heard from Amy and they'll do the official move from Sydney on the 22nd. A frantic rush. They have to fit in all the children's Christmas parties in three days as well as packing their stuff. However, Dwayne said they'll just bring the necessities, then he can go back and forth to organise the rest. They have plenty of time. Of course, they will stay at my place for Christmas Eve and so will Fe. I'm really excited.

Pam, Gaye and I went searching for a nice Christmas tree. Mum offered me her plastic one, but most of the leaves had dropped off and it looked really pathetic. I said

I'd decided to have a real tree this Christmas. Then of course we had the old argument about how real trees shed their pine needles everywhere and were a nuisance to get rid of. Anyway, we found a lovely tree. I've got it in a bucket of sand, and I've also anchored it to the mantelpiece. Can't have it falling over and squashing Dakota and Sydney.

I'm going to cook a big turkey with all the trimmings. I'll do a ham on the bone, too, with cloves and a fruit glaze. But I've cheated with the pudding and bought a large one from Peg-down-the-road. She's selling them to help the seniors raise money for a kitchen make-over in the club rooms. She said they'd made over a hundred puddings, boiled in cloths the old-fashioned way, and she's all puddinged out.

Sometimes I look at James's urn on the mantelpiece and wonder if he'd be proud of Fe and Amy, and of what I've achieved. You know, Lucy, if you'd asked me three years ago to rip up carpets, and build a deck and run a small business with two other women, I'd have laughed in your face.

Must go. Enjoy your honeymoon. A hug for Colin.

Love as always, Cath xx

December 20

DEAR JANE,

Just a quick email. Can you spare a few hours tomorrow to help us paint a lounge-room and dining-room? I know your speciality is gardens, but I'm sure you can wield a paint brush. I always thought you had lots of hidden talents. Anyway, it's an emergency job and has to be done before Christmas. So let me know if you can manage the time. Things are frantic.

Love Cath xx

December 20

DEAR FE,

Sorry this is a muddled email and you're just getting my thoughts as they spill out. I am really thrilled that you got the job with Dwayne's company. Heavens, it was all very quick, wasn't it? And so close to Christmas. Obviously you have just the skills they need.

Do you have an actual start date? Anyway, congratulations. I am very proud of you.

Love from Mum xx

December 20

Dear Lucy,

You're not going to believe this, but Fe got that job. Isn't it wonderful?

On Christmas Day, if people don't eat all the nibbles here, we can recycle them for your barbecue. Just as well we left the flares in the garden after the wedding, isn't it? They create a lovely ambience.

Speaking of ambience, here's a funny Christmas story. When four of Santa's elves got sick, Santa began to get behind schedule. Then Mrs Claus told him that her parents were coming to visit. This stressed Santa even more.

When he went to harness the reindeer, he found that two of them had jumped the fence and disappeared. More stress. Then when he began to load the sleigh he dropped his sack and toys went everywhere.

Santa went into the house for a soothing cup of tea. But he dropped the teapot and it smashed into hundreds of pieces. Just then the doorbell rang and Santa trudged to open it. There was a little angel with a great big Christmas tree. The angel said cheerfully, 'Merry Christmas, Santa. Isn't it a lovely day? I have a beautiful tree for you. Where would you like to put it?

And so began the tradition of the little angel on top of the Christmas tree

See you on Christmas Day.

Love from Cath xx

December 20

DEAR AMY

Yes, Fe getting the job with Dwayne's company is just fantastic. I love the idea of two girls living close enough to see each other regularly.

No, don't bring anything, it's enough drama travelling here with the children. Just come as you are. And don't worry about a high-chair and cot. I can borrow everything from Peg-down-the-road.

Do you need me to come and help you unpack and get settled on the 22nd?

Love from your mother xx

December 20,

DEAR ROBERT AND HELENE,

So sorry to hear that your girls won't be home for Christmas. Of course you're most welcome to come to lunch at my place. And then the party moves to Colin's house for an evening barbecue. It will be a wonderful Christmas, even though James won't be there.

Love from Cath

December 21

Dear Jane

I know, I know, I hated the red walls and slate grey too, but that's what the client wanted. Anyway, we did it. Thanks so much for your help. I know you're more into gardening, but I can see that you have definite talent as a painter (joke).

Of course, Bryan would be most welcome here on Christmas Day, but it's nice that he wants to help out at the rehab centre as a volunteer. Christmas can certainly be a bad time for folk without families. Or for people with families that fight all the time. Which makes me glad that I have my family. And of course I understand that you'll be spending Christmas Day in Ballarat with your relatives.

See you for pre-Christmas lunch at Antipasto's with the girls on Wednesday.

Love from Cath xx

December 23

Dear Lucy,

Yes, Amy and family are installed in Camberwell. Fe and I drove to the supermarket to stock up the fridge and cupboards so they wouldn't have to worry about food. Fe and I had done last-minute things at the house to make it nice and welcoming. Big bowls of fresh flowers in all the rooms, aired the place, that sort of thing. And we made a pile of sandwiches and set the table. Then we drove out to the airport to pick up Amy and the children. After lunch Dakota and Sydney had their naps and the girls headed straight for the pool, and when we finally left at five they all seemed very happy with their new surroundings.

All we need now is for Dwayne to love his new job, the girls to make some new friends, and Amy to settle into being a Melbourne housewife. She thinks that eventually she'll get a part-time job, but for now she's quite happy to stay home with the little ones. I can travel up once a week and babysit so she can go out and about. I think she thought it would be more often, but with Simply Handywomen there simply isn't enough time in my life. Still, I'll see them all a lot more than I ever did when they were in Sydney, which will be lovely.

No, I still haven't told Bob how I felt after he kissed

me. I'm content to let things drift along. And don't you dare interfere! What will be will be and I'm not sure that I want a full-on partner in my life. And he's made no moves or tried to put his arm round me or kiss me again. Maybe I imagined the spark between us, which is why you mustn't say anything to him. I don't want to look like a fool. No more on that subject, please.

Yes, Fe is still going out with David as far as I know – after all, it's only a couple of weeks! But I don't think it's anything serious at the moment.

Must go. Hugs to Colin, see you the day after tomorrow.

Love as always Cath xx

December 23

Dear Jane,

Here's the Sticky Marmalade and Date Cake recipe I promised you. It's easy to make and I think it's better than traditional Christmas cake. It'll be perfect as your contribution on Christmas Day.

1 cup prunes, chopped and seeded (or dried apricots if you prefer, but you really can't notice the prunes!)

1 cup dates, chopped and pitted (you can't notice them either!)

½ cup each sultanas and currants

1 cup water

275 gm butter

1 × 395 gm tin condensed milk

4 tblsp cumquat marmalade (or jam, but marmalade is best)

1 cup plain flour

1 cup SR flour

Put the fruit in a saucepan with the water, butter, condensed milk and 3 tblsp of the marmalade. Simmer for 5 minutes, then cool a bit. Stir in the flours. Place in a greased floured cake tin (or line it with baking paper), then lay a sheet of baking paper or foil over the tin so the cake doesn't brown too much. Bake it at 170° C for 2¼ hours.

Remove from the oven, take off the paper or foil, and leave to cool for 10 minutes. Turn out onto a wire rack. Brush the remaining marmalade over (heat it first). Rich and delicious, but also good for you.

Have a lovely Christmas. See you in the New Year.

Love from Cath xx.

December 24

Dear Fe,

I must say I feel rather hurt that Bob met with you and Amy behind my back and none of you said a word about it. And I wouldn't have even found out at all except Dakota told me on the phone that you'd all gone out and that Lucy and Colin were babysitting.

It's right on Christmas and I don't want to feel upset with anyone. And now I do. I am extremely upset that you've decided to stay in Melbourne tonight. And now Amy and Dwayne aren't coming till tomorrow either – Amy said the children are overtired and fractious and they need an early night.

What's going on? I was all excited and now I feel very sad and upset and . . . flat.

Mum

December 24

Dear Fe

All right, I will ask Bob!

Mum

December 24

Dear Lucy

Something weird is going on. First, Bob had dinner with Fe and Amy and Dwayne. And no one told me. And now no one's coming to stay tonight. I feel betrayed. And upset. And confused. You must know something, because you and Colin were babysitting. Tell me what's going on!

Love from Cath xx

December 24

Dear Lucy,

What do you mean you don't know what's going on, and that I should ask Bob or Amy or Fe? Fe won't answer her phone, Amy's clammed up and Bob seems to have disappeared off the face of the earth. He's not at work. He's not at home. I hope he's not dead under a bridge somewhere. All this is really spoiling my Christmas – and it's only Christmas Eve.

Cath

December 25

DEAR FE

It's six on Christmas morning and I hope you look at your emails before you set off.

You little imp. You knew! But I'm so happy that I can forgive you. Now I understand that Bob was seeking your help. It must've been very confusing for him if he saw me as blowing hot and cold, friendly one minute and distancing myself the next. I told him I was scared I'd scare him away if I started getting affectionate or flirted with him.

You can tell Ali thanks for the thought but I couldn't have coped if this had all happened on top of a ferris wheel. Or on top of anything, for that matter. Sitting in my lounge-room by the Christmas tree in the lovely mellow lamplight was just perfect. And now I understand why you all stayed away and Pam and Gaye didn't turn up for drinks as arranged. Just dear Bob.

It seems everyone was in on what was happening except me. But I'm not mad at you all. I think it's lovely that you all conspired to get Bob to tell me how he felt. Otherwise we probably would have toddled along as best friends for years, loving each other but not game to say anything.

Well, I've got the turkey stuffed and I'm just pottering around. Bob helped me set the table last night. Not very romantic, but very practical.

Do you know, I'm sure your father would approve of this, too. He always liked Bob. I had a little farewell talk to his urn this morning, and I've put it away in a safe place in his great-grandpa's old sea chest. It's time for a new beginning.

Must go, see you both very soon,

Love from Mum xx

P.S. Remember to bring the bon-bons.

December 25

Dear Lucy,

I don't know if you'll be looking at your emails on Christmas morning. It's too early to phone you with my news. It's only six-thirty.

Last night, Bob told me that he loves me. I haven't told the others, but he also wants to marry me!

But that's further down the track. He'd asked Fe and Amy whether he should tell me that he loves me because he was frightened I'd laugh at him or something equally crass. In fact, Fe said he was very apprehensive that I might bolt the other way. And when Fe told him that she was sure I was in love with him but wasn't game to say so, he was over the moon.

And before you even ask, no, he didn't stay the night. We both want everything to happen slowly in the old-fashioned way. A proper courtship. I'm still in shock. But walking on Cloud Nine. What a wonderful Christmas present, the best I could have. And today, with my family around me, and tonight with my friends and my family at your barbecue. What more could anyone want?

See you tonight.

Love as always, Cath xx

December 26

DEAR FE,

Thank you for being with Bob and me on Christmas Day and giving me one of the best Christmases I've ever had.

Bob and I are going to spend a quiet day at home. The antique diamond and ruby pin he gave me is just beautiful, isn't it?

No, we haven't talked about a formal engagement or a wedding yet.

We'll probably watch the start of the Sydney to Hobart yacht race on TV. See you soon,

Love from Mum xx

December 26

DEAR AMY AND DWAYNE AND CHILDREN

That was one of the best Christmas Days I have ever had. Apart from Dakota coming into the kitchen with a handful of glass slithers and announcing that the jingle bell had 'bit' him. And I didn't mind at all that Virginia and Georgia wanted to phone Marla three times.

I'm sorry that Grandpa lost the plot and asked you to give him a shower. I think he thought you were Brief Respite. And special thanks to Dwayne for his quick thinking when Grandma got the wheel of her chair caught in the table cloth.

Well, I didn't put coins in the Christmas pudding in case someone choked and we had to rush them to hospital. Too risky. It was better to pop them under people's pudding plates, don't you think?

And Lucy's barbecue was wonderful, wasn't it? I'm glad Grandpa wasn't there. He would have gone all tropical again. By the time the Christmas festivities were over at my place, both of them were exhausted.

Speaking of barbecues, thank you for my new gas grill and hot plate. How about a New Year's Eve barbecue at my place and then afterwards we can take the children down to the foreshore and watch the fireworks? I don't think Fe will be able to come. I remember her saying something about a party in Melbourne. It would be wonderful if you and the children came and stayed the night. Remember how we used to sleep outdoors if it was hot? We could do that. No mosquitoes here.

Yes, Bob is a wonderful man and I am so happy that we love each other.

Love from your mother xx

December 27

Dear Lucy,

We had a lovely time at the barbecue, so thanks to both of you.

The young ones skinny-dipping was a bit much, though, don't you think? Just as well Amy and Dwayne had gone home with the kids by that stage. And that Robert and Helene were busy inside trying to impress some of Colin's friends.

Yes, I love my ruby and diamond pin and I love Bob. You said that you didn't know the secret. Well, you and I must have been the only ones. Bob apparently had a heart-to-heart with Gaye and Pam, too. Just as well everyone said 'Go for it, Bob', or we'd still be puddling along.

Well, it's nearly the end of the year. And what a year. Fe going off on her own, having adventures and developing into an independent young woman. Amy and Dwayne moving to Melbourne. All the ups and downs with my parents . . . Amazing when you think of it.

And you meeting Colin after all those years. The whirlwind courtship, and your beautiful wedding. Jane coming out of her shell and finding Life Without Derek. Pam, Gaye and I starting Simply Handywomen. And Bob and I falling in love.

Who would have thought that so much could happen, just in one year.

I wonder what next year will bring us?

Love as always, Cath xx

Acknowledgements

First, I would like to thank my dear friends Julie Watts and Janet Raunjak from Penguin Books, who actually thought my emails to them were funny and interesting enough to have potential as a book. Originally the book was based on emails between me and my daughter Fe, but it ended up a novel rather than an e-autobiography.

I would also like to thank Bob Sessions at Penguin for his faith in my ability to write an adult novel and for allowing Julie, Janet and I to work together on the initial drafts. To publisher Clare Forster, thank you for loving *The Femails* and giving it so much undivided attention and enthusiasm. Without my two wonderful editors, Meredith Rose and Sarah Dawson, the book would not have been so well shaped and crafted. Your editorial skills are astounding: thank you, you both 'done real good'.

To Miriam Rosenbloom, thank you for designing such an appealing cover. To Sally Bateman, Felicity Irvine and Daniel Ruffino, thanks for working so hard to promote the book.

ALSO FROM PENGUIN BOOKS

THE LIST OF ALL ANSWERS

Peter Goldsworthy

Ranging from the early comic sketches to the disturbing brilliance of his recent stories, this outstanding collection reinforces Peter Goldsworthy's reputation as a modern master of short fiction. Simultaneously light and dark, unsettling and amusing, his stories leave indelible traces in the memory. A writer's writer, he is also never less than compellingly readable.

THE ALPHABET SISTERS

Monica McInerney

Sisters are always there for each other . . . aren't they?

Anna, Bett and Carrie were childhood singing stars – the Alphabet Sisters. As adults they haven't spoken for years. Not since Bett's fiance left her for another sister . . .

Now Lola, their larger-than-life grandmother, summons them home for a birthday extravaganza and a surprise announcement. But just as the rifts begin to close, the Alphabet Sisters face a test none of them ever imagined.

An unforgettable story of three women who learn that begin true to themselves means being true to each other.

KNITTING

Anne Bartlett

Friendship, grief and unexpected grace – a novel to gladden the heart

It's been ten months since Jack died, and Sandra, a tightly wound academic, copes with her grief by immersing herself in the history of textiles. When she and Martha, a gifted knitter, meet over an unconscious body on the footpath, the unlikely threads of their lives become entangled. Sandra invites Martha to join her in a professional collaboration, but what begins as a working relationship becomes something deeply personal. Martha seems at ease with herself, in spite of her own experience of grief. But what does she carry around in those three large bags?

'Reading *Knitting* is an experience as sensual and mystical as plunging your hands into skeins of wool and colour . . . a joyful narrative of creating and connecting.'

— Sena Jeter Naslund, author of *Ahab's Wife*

THE ROSE NOTES

M. Andrea Mayes

Some secrets can destroy you, others can set you free . . .

Charming, infuriating Dobie Kinnear, widower and manipulator extraordinaire, is battling to retain his wits, his authority and his only daughter, Pearl.

Pearl, a hostage to her ageing father's needs, fiercely resents her role as Dobie's unofficial housekeeper. The years are passing on their southern Riverina farm, and still her life lacks meaning or purpose. She loves the farm with a passion but, tending her rose garden, she dreams of escape.

Then a stranger comes to Mamerbrook Farm bearing a secret from the past and a gift for the future. Along with an old scrapbook of roses, a hitchhiking angel, and an onion farmer with a knack for rescuing people, he will turn their world upside down . . . and change their lives for ever.